Alexander Raleigh

The Book of Esther : its practical lessons and dramatic scenes

Alexander Raleigh

The Book of Esther : its practical lessons and dramatic scenes

ISBN/EAN: 9783337305857

Printed in Europe, USA, Canada, Australia, Japan

Cover: Foto ©Andreas Hilbeck / pixelio.de

More available books at **www.hansebooks.com**

THE

Book of Esther

ITS PRACTICAL LESSONS AND
DRAMATIC SCENES

BY

ALEXANDER RALEIGH, D.D.

KENSINGTON

EDINBURGH
ADAM AND CHARLES BLACK
1880

PREFACE.

THE Author of these Lectures has chanced to see of late in some secular prints which he respects, a very disparaging estimate expressed of this Book of Esther. Remembering that he had, not long ago, spent the Sunday evenings of more than two months, not unhappily to himself, and, as he was assured at the time, not without instruction and profit to his people, in lecturing through this Book: recollecting also that he had been asked by not a few of them to put the Lectures into print, partly for the sake of the interesting history, and yet more for the worth of the lessons drawn from it — he has been

induced (and for other reasons as well which
need not be stated) to reconsider the case,
and to give now to the world, or rather to
that very small part of it which will concern
itself with the matter, this little volume,
which now no one is asking for, but which
the Author modestly hopes may not be un-
welcome to some who have had favour to his
writings, and possibly also to some beyond.
The Lectures are what is called " popular "—
one hopes in no inferior sense.   Still, they
were written to be spoken, and not in the
writing of them intended to be read.   The
style therefore is in a few places perhaps a
little affluent.   But the Author has not
applied the pruning - knife, or sought to
change the style, for indeed, he means
nothing more, nor perhaps could he mean
anything greater, by the publication of this
little book, than a wider preaching.

CONTENTS.

LECTURE I.

THE FEAST.

THIS Book of Esther stands in the canon of Holy Scripture. But it is no secret that its place there has been challenged. Even Luther " expressed a wish that the Book of Esther was not contained in the Bible." This wish of the great Reformer was, no doubt, grounded on those characteristics of the book, negative and positive, which give it a uniqueness not altogether pleasant.

'Tis said, for instance, that it reads like an Oriental story or romance. 'Tis a tale for the traveller's tent ; or for any listening evening group, and by some mistake must have found its way into the sacred record. But it is difficult to see any force in this objection, since this is exactly what it professes to be——a tale, an eastern tale, and full of eastern imagery, as far at least as the facts of the exterior history go.   May not God write any portion of human history, transpiring in any part of the world, if He sees it needful to do so for the instruction of mankind ?   The questions of real importance are such as these :——How is the history written ?   What instructions are given in it ?   What lessons are intended to be drawn by the readers ?

"True," say the objectors, "but there is no sound instruction in the book at all.   The personages introduced are not great, are not even good morally.   The characters delineated are all of a worldly type ; or, if the religious tone is found in any of them, it is unusually low, hardly recognisable as a religious tone at all.   An eastern despot putting out his personal will as the supreme law of a vast empire, and at times turning all his power and wealth into means for the gratification of sensual appetites and wicked passions !   A malignant prime minister who can plot the destruction of a whole race who have done no wrong, and whom he is bound to protect, because *one* of their number has refused to do him honour! A Jew without patriotism, and without much conscience, or he would not, of his own choice, be found sitting at the gate of a heathen sovereign! A fair woman with surely no beauty of soul, or anything in her nature highly sensitive, else she never would have followed the advice given by her wily relative, under no prompting of danger, and solely with purposes of ambition ;—are these the characters which God would be likely to select and describe for the instruction of the world ?"

There is no force in this objection. It is founded in radical mistake. It goes on the supposition that all the characters delineated on the sacred page must be saintly ; and that all the historic scenes described in the Bible must have direct and immediate bearing on the fortunes of the kingdom of God ; and that this must be made so plain that every one shall be able to see it at a glance. Whereas the fact is, that all through the Bible there is a perfectly impartial and unselective delineation of human character, the good and the evil intermixed in the picture as historic truth requires, to say nothing of the circumstance that some of the saints are not very saintly. The most valuable lessons of wisdom, and some of the most important moral inferences, may be drawn from the darkest or from the poorest scenes of human history. God being judge, we need to know Cain as well as Abel, Jezebel as well as Miriam, the bad kings as much as the good. The loving broken-hearted women and the scowling Pharisees must be together at the very cross! Granted that in this book of Esther there is no clear instance of human goodness of the higher stamp; not the less, as I hope we shall see, may the design and the influence of the book on the whole be good.

It is really but a small objection which has been made to this book, that there is no mention in it of the name of God; and perhaps, to this the quaint but not unwise reply of Matthew Henry is enough, "that though *the name* of God be not in it, His finger is." A religious discourse may have little or no formal mention of the name of Christ, and yet may take hearer or reader very near the cross; while another which is full of the name may yet be empty and vacant of its power.

The book is canonical because it forms part of the Hebrew Scriptures, which all Christians receive of the Jews, which our Lord used or sanctioned every time He went into a Jewish synagogue.

The author of the book is not known. It takes its name from the Jewish female whose fortunes are described, not, as we apprehend, because they are *intrinsically* worthy of this perpetual elevation and honour, but because they are inseparably associated with the fortunes of the Jewish people, and, by their means, with the history of the world. Esther herself, however, is not the writer of the book ; Mordecai perhaps ; or, a little more probably, Ezra. It matters not. It would be pleasant to know, but we are scarcely the poorer for not knowing.

The time is about 480 years B.C. Under the good Edict of Darius, the captive Jews had returned to their own land. But they had not *all* returned. Many of them were content to stay in the country where they were captives, and where most of them had been born. But they are not forsaken or forgotten of God. What a Providence is

over them this wonderful story makes known;
and the book is to be held in everlasting
remembrance, if only as showing to all ages
and to all peoples how much the Heavenly
care and love are concerned with those who
themselves have little or no care to keep
God's commandments.   The Shepherd seeks
the sheep, watches over them in untended
fields, and throws around them unseen protections in the wilderness where they wander.

THE FEAST.

And now we may begin.   " It came to pass
in the days of Ahasuerus "—Ahasuerus was an
official name of the Persian kings—" who
reigned from India even unto Ethiopia, over
an hundred and seven and twenty provinces,
—when he sat on the throne of his kingdom."
Historical research has made it certain that
this Ahasuerus is none other than the famous
Xerxes, the Persian monarch who makes
such a figure in Grecian history.   This is he
who came in eastern pomp and magnificence,
and with his myriad numbers, into Greece,
intending to subdue and destroy it as a

nation by annexing it to his own dominions, but who, as secular history informs us, suffered complete and ignominious defeat at Salamis.

"He sat on the throne of his kingdom, which was in Shushan the palace." Shushan or Susa was the principal royal residence of the Persian monarchs. It was situated on the Choaspes, about 200 miles south-east of Babylon. He sat on the throne, evidently robed and in royal state, peoples and provinces in their representatives beholding the glory and rendering homage. This habit of royalty is highly characteristic of the man. Herodotus and Æschylus tell us how he sat on his royal throne, silver-footed, and saw the world-famed martyrdom of Leonidas and his brave three hundred Spartans, and the indomitable courage of Themistocles and his Grecian armament at Salamis. The issue of the conflict was immensely and appallingly different from what he had expected : and it is not too much to say that the whole world and all the after ages are debtor to those tremendous, death-defying Greeks. Well, there he sat to see a victory, and lo! it was changed, as by celestial powers, into an overwhelming defeat. The affrighted monarch rushed from that Athenian hill, and fled with his scattered forces in dismay. But there he " sat," as he " sits " here. It is the same man although here is neither battle nor danger. He is in the heart of his own kingdom and on the height of his glory. All his princes and servants are gathered. The nobles and princes of the provinces are before him.

He has ordained a feast for them. But the feast is really to his own power and pride, for while they feast through all those long days, he is " showing them the riches of his glorious kingdom, and the honour of his excellent majesty."

There is good reason to suppose that this feast was held on the occasion of his projected invasion of Greece. To fill the minds of his captains with confidence, and to fire his soldiers with military ardour, he makes all this vain display and provides this munificence of self-indulgence. If this be so, with how little favourable result when the brunt of the struggle came! Yet what other result than that which actually came could be reasonably expected? Real courage and endurance are bred of much harder conditions than these. How are real men made? and how are they made ready for any manly thing of more than common difficulty? By feasting on rich viands? By drinking wine and looking on it when it is red in the cup? By nights of revelry? By gazing on the outside shows of life? By sinking into voluptuous ease? Never since the world began have manhood and courage sprung of such things as these, although in a few rare instances they may have passed through them unbroken and not much defiled. The Greeks were comparatively few, and comparatively poor; and their country had no vast harvest-bearing plains. They were fighting for rocks and mountains and seas. But those mountains and seas were the symbols and the guardians of their *liberty*. It was for the defence of that they fought. Every heart was steeled with the high resolve that, Come life, come death to them as individuals, the last asylum of freedom should be defended, the future home of freedom made secure. Only in such a spirit could they have scattered and driven away like smoke these Persian hosts.

And there can be no doubt that this great law runs through the whole of human life and history. It affects not only nations and communities as such, but families and individuals. Those who are fed from the breasts of abundance, cushioned on the lap of luxury, feasted with shows of life, exhausted with ceremonies, may get indeed by such means easy, gliding manners, a politic and willowy softness, convenient enough for life's ever-shifting scenes and necessities. But they do not get by such means an inward courage or an outward strength for the harder, higher duties, and the better possibilities of life. No. Stress of difficulty, hard work, plain fare, the touch of privation even, the wolf seen from the window, if not quite at the door ; these things make men, or, at least, have much more to do with the making of men, than their opposites.

The length of the feast is remarkable. "An hundred and fourscore days." A feast continuing for even three or four days would be onerous and wearisome to any of us, or to any modern monarch. The explanation probably is that *this was a festive time.* " It was the custom of the Persians to combine great councils with great festivities." Ahasuerus had just won great victories in Egypt. The Egyptian campaign was preceded by solemn councils and muster of troops. The Grecian campaign has a like beginning, although, as we know, a very different ending. But this accounts for the long stretch of time which has been regarded by some as fabulous. The time was really occupied in consultation. The chiefs of the countries and provinces forming the one great empire came into a council of war. The story of the past would be narrated to many a chief, to many a company. Objections and difficulties would be obviated. The advantages of such an expedition would be held out to encourage the spirits of any who might be flagging and disposed to draw back.

At the very end of the time—during the last seven days—this feast culminated, and then overflowed into unbounded beneficence. It became a feast to all, great and small, who were in the capital. For seven days the whole population was entertained with sump-

tuous and royal magnificence. Why dwell
on the splendour, the wonderful decorations,
the rich hangings of the pavilions, the silver
rings, the pillars of marble, the couches of gold
and silver resting upon a pavement of red,
and blue, and white, and black marble?
Every guest treated like a very monarch,
privileged to drink royal wine in vessels of
gold, according to the state of the king, the
vessels being diverse one from another—that
is, never used more than once—replaced as
soon as they were emptied by vessels of other
form and pattern. It is a wonderful scene.
There is nothing morally great about it: there
never can be about mere feasting and splendour. But neither, so far as we can see, is
there anything morally wrong in it, as these
things are judged among men. Neither
morally stimulating nor elevating intellectually, it may yet perhaps be called one of the
artistic triumphs of the time—or even the
highest of them all.

Nothing morally great, we said, in the feast
itself, and yet here is a precept or rule for
the conduct of it, of quite unusual moral
worth, the principle of moderation. This

may be reckoned a sort of canon law of the Persian feast. It is put out, indeed, only in the negative form. There is no actual inculcation of the great virtue of moderation or sobriety. But the law has, clearly, a leaning that way. "The drinking was according to the law. None did compel." The king had expressly appointed "that they should do according to every man's pleasure." Of course there is the question whether, if some man's "pleasure" should take him beyond the bounds of temperance and propriety, any restraint would be put upon him? It seems as if there would be. The enforcement of that part of the rule, if it existed, was probably left with the "officers of the house." The dangerous time was at the end of a feast, as we shall see. Meantime, it is enough to observe that there is to be no compulsion; the inebriating cup is not to be pressed on the unwilling guest. That custom apparently had been but too common among the Persians and their imitators. It is not entirely, however, in moral recoil that sanction is thus given in law to the better practice. There is a touch of political prudence it it. For here at the feast are princes from all parts, with their retainers and tribes.   There are men here from the mountains who are famous for their temperance and for the strictness and simplicity of their manners.   Such men would not be won, but disgusted rather and alienated from the royal cause, by anything like Bacchanalian excess.   In prudence, therefore, as well as from, possibly, higher motive, the principle of temperance must have the reinforcement of public law.

It is humiliating to remember that no long time has elapsed in this country since the very same objectionable and repulsive habit against which this public law of the Persians was directed, prevailed in some of the social circles of this country.   It was a point of hospitality to press the bottle even on the unwilling guest.   The generous host hardly felt that he had done his duty until his guests were reeling, and if some of them were under the table the triumph of his beneficence was complete.   You might easily cull from the poets of the last century, both of England and Scotland, descriptions and allusions pointing to a state of things which, happily has now passed away. This, indeed, is our reason for dwelling on such a subject— repulsive enough in itself,—for even a few moments. It is always helpful to observe any signs of a real progress, and, undoubtedly, in the course of a generation or two, we have in this particular made very great progress. Within the whole sphere of what is called society, anything approaching compulsion would not be tolerated, and in fact is never attempted.

Whether we do not, on a wider scale, as a people in fact, and with the force of law, practise compulsion still, and that on the weakest and most helpless part of our people, is a very serious question, and one which, to say the least, we cannot answer with the same confidence. If places where drink is sold to the common people are multiplied much beyond the reasonable needs of the community ; if exceptional privileges are given to the sellers ; if their houses, with many exits and entrances, are planted in the most conspicuous spots ; if they burn the brightest lights in the streets, and are allowed to keep open long after other trades and industries are closed

and silent, does not all this and more of the
same kind amount to a sort of compulsion
to working-people, and trades-people, and
thoughtless young people of both sexes?
If *the spirit* of that old Persian law were
expressed in our own legislation about drink,
it would, as we cannot help feeling, be all
the better for the morals and manners of
our time, for the sobriety of the working-
classes, and for the safety of the young.
" Men are not made virtuous by Act of Parliament " has grown to be a kind of axiom on
this and some other subjects ; and many a
one rides off on it, easily and gaily, as though
he had performed some feat in logic.   But
the axiom is one which ought to be disputed.
It is not broadly and roundly true.   Indeed
a part of it is untrue ; for Acts of Parliament,
when they are wise and suitable to the people
for whom they are framed, do help, instrumentally, to make men virtuous.   So Acts of
Parliament, when they are unwise and evil,
help, instrumentally, to make men vicious.
When temptations and inducements to excess
are made too strong for the feeble resistance
they meet with, and made so partly by legis-

lation, is it not clear that the State herself becomes a temptress, and to that extent does "compel"? She makes the law under which —in whatever way the responsibility may be shared—there are so many victims. She gathers the tax which intemperance pays to sustain her magnificence and power. She must therefore have some corresponding ability to promote goodness and morality in their exterior forms. She can refuse to tempt ; or to sanction temptation. She can keep the path of virtue and obedience, as far as it is in her care, open. In one word, as we have it on the highest authority, she can be "the minister of God" to men "for good."

So much we have thought it right to say in contravention of the dictum of the let-alone philosophy which is so much applied to this and some kindred subjects. But we cordially assent to the view that virtue and goodness in the deeper sense are first of all from above—from the Father of lights, from the untempted, untempting God, all-generous, ever-merciful—and then that in earthly form they are the result and product of the free action and mutual intercourse of human

C

minds.   Let the moral and intellectual power of the community, in its full force, come to the rescue.   Direct conflict with evil can only take us a certain length even if it be successful.   The inculcation and the production of goodness among our fellow-men will take us at once into illimitable fields, and set us on a pathway of progress unending.   When we have large increase of knowledge among the people, some corresponding elevation of social sentiment, and some refinement of taste, and some improvement in the structure of houses, and amusements which are not corrupting and yet are really amusing—we may hope confidently to see the same process taking place among the masses of the people, in relation to temperance, which has been accomplished so largely among the higher classes.   It is a vast and various problem.   It is a long question.   We can only do our own part by adopting sound principles, and, still more, by the uniform practice of moderation in all things, because we are of those who believe that "the Lord is at hand."   Whether we eat, therefore, or drink, or whatsoever we do, let us do all to His glory—"using this world

as not abusing it," for the fashion of it
"passeth away."

How has the fashion of the world passed
away from that Persian capital! the palaces!
the gardens! the pavilions! the tesselated
pavements! the rich couches! the golden
goblets ! the flowing banquet ! the gay
throngs! the grand monarch! the mustering
armies? They have all gone like a dream.
The Persian people now are among the
poorest and most abject in the world. And
their country?—will hardly support them.
So fades all exterior glory. So all visible
things do pass away. And England's grandeur
is but a part of the ever-vanishing procession,
the whole description of which is this—"the
world passeth away." But if we embody the
principle of moderation in our life, and
"walk by faith and not by sight," and take
the word and will of God as the light unto
our feet, and the lamp unto our path, for
solitude and company, for the funeral and
for the feast, then we surmount the poor
pageant in which, outwardly, we are moving
figures; we cast anchor within the veil, lay up
treasure where it cannot be lost, live in the

life that cannot die, and with God and all the good " abide for ever."

And now may we try to speak for a few moments of that other feast of which we often read in this same Bible, and at which, even here, amid the changes and the shadows, we may all sit down ? Where is it spread ? " On this mountain." On what mountain ? On no mountain in particular now. Jerusalem has given her name to every mountain and every hill ; wherever heights arise from plains, or plains sink from heights : wherever suns shine, or even only stars for half the year : wherever waters run, wherever breezes blow, is God's Jerusalem—His city of peace and presence. On this mountain of His own grace and manifestation, the Lord has " made unto all people a feast of fat things "—the richest blessings which He can give, or we receive—forgiveness for sin, which else were our ruin : converting and creating grace to make all things new, to make the young child-heart beat even in the old man's breast : the spirit of adoption that will lift us up as on dove's wings, towards the fatherliness of God and the homeliness of heaven : God and

His love: Christ and His fulness: Promises spread out like viands: protections standing around us like walls and towers: prospects stretching before us, away towards the infinite, eternal—ever-blessed life—"a feast of fat things" indeed, "of fat things full of marrow" —not only the best in quality, but the best of the best we may have if we will—a feast rich and full with all the mercy and all the munificence of God. But how shall we find admission to the feast? By coming. But can we come without an invitation? Here is the invitation as surely from God as the ten commandments were, which were written with His own finger, or as it would be if an angel from heaven gave it at this moment into your own hand: " Ho every one that thirsteth, come ye to the waters." " Buy and eat." Buy—not by giving something for something else, something human for something divine, but only by asking, by holding out the hand. That, on our part, is the purchase-money. Therefore the thing attained is said to be " without money and without price." " Eat ye that which is good." " Let your soul delight itself in fatness "—the best of the

best.   Sit down if you will under the King's
shadow and let His fruit be sweet unto your
taste.   Let Him bring you to his banqueting-
house, where His banner over you will be
love.

Then life itself becomes in some measure a
banquet.   The feast is continual—bread of
adversity sometimes given, waters of sorrow
sometimes wrung out, yet marvellously changed
and mingled with happier elements, and
made by divine blessing into living bread,
with which the soul is fed.   The good conscience makes the merry heart; and "the
merry heart," the wise man tells us, "hath a
continual feast."   Saith one with whose words
we close,—speaking of Him whose heart is
sincere and whose conscience is quiet—" Be
the air clear or cloudy, he enjoys a continual
serenity, and continually sits at that blessed
feast whereat the blessed angels are cooks
and butlers, as Luther hath it, and the three
persons in trinity, gladsome guests—all other
feasts to this are stark hunger.   It is a full
feast: a lasting feast: not for a day as that
of Nabal: not for seven days as that of
Samson: no, nor of nine score days as that

of Ahasuerus, but a durable continual feast
without intermission of solace or interruption
of society "—and all this only a preparation
for the great Epiphany, when you shall feast
indeed.

LECTURE II.

HOW THE FEAST ENDED.

WELL had it been for Ahasuerus if he and his courtiers and tributary princes had been as careful to maintain personal sobriety as they were to enforce the admirable law of liberty leaning to moderation, which sufficiently protected the soberly inclined among his guests. It is but too evident that, as the great feast culminated and drew to a close, the drinking was deeper and the restraint less severe. At any rate "the heart of the king was merry with wine." The councils had prospered. The great expedition was to go forward in due time; and proud Greece to be vanquished, and made subject to the mighty empire.

The feast has come to its last day. " Swell high the song.   Let the wine flow.   Fill the goblet to the brim, and quaff it to the honour of the great monarch ! "   If he himself drinks deeply, although the law is still in force that " none must compel " another to do so, there will be plenty to follow the evil example. For, let a king sit in a tavern, or wallow in the mire—he will not lack even *noble* companionship.   No doubt on this occasion many of the princes drank as their master did ; and talked of their queens, and wives, and concubines.   In some way, in an evil moment, the thought took possession of the mind of Ahasuerus that the royal glory of this supreme night would shine with its very highest lustre, if he might call Vashti the queen royal—*the* queen among all the queens, for there was always one, not only first in the monarch's heart, but first also in law, and place, and dignity ; and Vashti is *the* queen-supreme over all women.   But it is not because she is first in law that she is wanted —as if to complete and grace some solemn resolution of the government ; it is because she is peerless in beauty—the very name

Vashti signifying "*beautiful woman.*" It is not chiefly because she wears the crown-royal, but rather because she outshines it—that she is wanted by the monarch now. In the simple but expressive phraseology of the narrative, he wishes to "show the people and the princes her beauty; for she was fair to look on." Is this thy love, O king! to the woman who of all women is dearest to thy heart! that thou wilt bring her forth from chaste retirement, and set her as a show before the rude gaze of drunken men! Than to persuade thee to this, the devil could do thee no more devilish service. But it is done. The evil thought has taken root. And the word of command is spoken. The seven chamberlains or eunuchs (whose very names are written down—showing that the historian is intimately acquainted with the particulars), are commanded to bring the queen.

The queen — where is she! Possibly presiding still at her own feast of the women; or more probably gone to her own apartments after it was over. On her startled ear fall the few words of the king's command. But who can describe the swift confusion of her thoughts? Surprise: anger: perhaps—who knows? one passing gleam of satisfaction, food to her woman's vanity — that she should be so desired—but soon chased away by rising indignation, indignation in its turn touched for a moment with the light of love, and held in check by the spirit of obedience.

But there is no time for reflection. The answer. The seven chamberlains wait. "Go, tell the king that I will not come!" "Vashti refused to come at the king's commandment." What the reason was that swayed her to this bold step, we are not told. Her motives may have been mixed. Perhaps she was tired with her own exertions. Perhaps she felt that for the time she was *not* beautiful, and would not look queenly. Perhaps she thought the summons too peremptory, and the bearers of it not dignified enough to come to her with such a message. We cannot certainly tell. All human motives are more or less mixed, and so were hers— but one feels bound to say that by far the most probable cause of her refusal was a deep sense of injury done to her womanhood, and of course to her queenliness, in this sud-

den call to show herself in such a company,
at such a time. This is certainly the impression we get from the narrative ; and, supposing it correct, it raises the question much
more easily stated than answered—"Was
Vashti justified in this refusal to show herself at the king's commandment?" We do
not get an answer to this question, when we
allow and even assert that the king was
utterly wrong in sending for her. Say that
in the hilarious excitement of the hour he
forgot his own dignity, and unwittingly did
foul scorn to one whom yet apparently he
sincerely loved. Was she, therefore, justified
in thus peremptorily setting at nought his
authority—and that before the princes, and before all the people? For no more conspicuous
rebellion could be made ; no greater slight
could be offered to the throne or to the man.
Was it absolutely necessary to do this?
Might not compliance have been better, on
the whole, and especially better in its moral
effects on the king himself? and on the
public sentiment as touching the laws of
married and domestic life? The Bible gives
no hint of the proper answer : and we are

left to answer it according to our lights ; or,
rather, one fears it will be according to our
individual tastes, our predilections, our pre-
judices, our passions, our domestic habits.
They say "an Englishman's house is his
castle," and in it he is a little king.   Here
and there, no doubt, might be found one
who is in the habit of demeaning himself in
monarchic style within the said castle, and
sending for Vashti quite imperiously, to receive
his commands and do his pleasure, when he
goes out and when he comes in.   Well, *he*
will be ready enough with an answer.   He
will hold that the queen in her divorce got
only her true deserts.   It never would do to
allow woman to take into her own hands a
liberty of black rebellion.   It would turn the
world upside down.   Wives are to obey their
husbands, not resist them, far less rule them.
The wife is the weaker vessel, and should
trust to her husband's protection, not seek to
protect herself.   The wife is the angel, and
ought to stand where she is set, for admiration, be it the public banquet or her own
fireside.   "I am quite clear on the point,"
says this lord and master, this little Ahasu-

erus in his own realm, "no queen for my house that will not submit and obey."

Then, on the other hand, if any one feels that if his house be a castle his wife keeps the key of it ; and does so perhaps largely with his own consent, because he is of an easy mind, or of indolent habit, or because he has an unaffected admiration of his wife's genius and capacity and moral worth ;—why, then, on the other hand, the answer of this man also is a foregone conclusion. Thus you see we are apt to answer a question like this by our prepossessions and habits.

Now, as this subject affects the very chief relations of human life, all married people and all families, it may not be without use to give here some brief consideration to the fixed principles, both scriptural and natural, which rule this question for all time. As regards the scriptural teaching, we are per-haps liable to think it in some points stronger and clearer than it is. It is never in one isolated text or passage that we shall find the whole and harmonious truth on any great subject. St. Paul, it is thought, has settled or has declared for ever the relation between the husband and the wife, and so clearly that there never can be any hesitation or uncertainty about it in the mind of a believing reader of the Scriptures.   The husband commands, the wife obeys.   " Wives, submit yourselves unto your own husbands." " As the Church is subject unto Christ, so let the wives be to their own husbands in everything."   Could anything be clearer?   Yet is it not the same St. Paul who says that in Christ Jesus there is neither Jew nor Greek, neither bond nor free, *neither male nor female*, for all are one in Him?   If it be said that we must limit and confine this oneness to the sphere in which it is alleged to exist, the same surely ought to be said with regard to the " subjections " of which the apostle treats in his Epistles to the Ephesians and Colossians.   There is in some things a fundamental equality between the sexes in the Christian kingdom.   There is in some things a fundamental difference which can only be expressed by such words as subordination, subjection, as applied to the woman.   Both ideas must be taken, and some others added to them which we need not stay to specify, and the whole must be duly considered before we can expect to get the full Christian teaching on the subject. The Christian teaching was hardly final, nor could be, in the Apostle Paul's time. We have now no "slave" servants, and we make insensible modifications—we cannot help it—in the applications of the Apostolic language to the servants of our own time. Woman's whole position is different from that in which she stood when the Christian Epistles were written. She has been elevated by Christianity, unspeakably, and we almost feel it to be treason against Christianity itself when the attempt is made to smite her down again by the strong-handed use of these New Testament texts.

Yet with all these allowances, and after considering all the elements of the case, it is clear, both from Scripture and in nature, that the husband, in the domestic economy, occupies the supreme position. The law of subordination, however interpreted, leaves him there. There is unity and equality in some things. There is reciprocal obligation in all things ; but still, out of these things, and coloured and limited by them, there arises the priority of the husband, the consequent subjection, although limited, of the wife. This is truly a divine appointment, but it is not made in an arbitrary manner, like, for instance, a positive institution of the Jews, which might be this way or that way with equal propriety—the thing deriving its sacred character chiefly from the fact of the appointment. Even a divine appointment could not make the wife supreme, human nature continuing what it is.

For one thing, woman is weaker than man physically, and supremacy goes with strength. All kinds of force have their ultimate source in God, and when He makes man permanently stronger than woman, no doubt He means some corresponding authority to rest where the permanent strength does. And so the Scriptures say. No doubt strength may be abused, is most shamefully abused in some instances, by the husband. But the way to prevent the abuse of strength is not, surely, to attempt to transfer its proper responsibilities to weakness? Weakness may be abused as much as strength, and in some ways even more. There is a certain authority that rests indefeasibly with the husband. There is a certain submission, or say compliance, which nature as well as Scripture requires of the wife. Shakespeare makes one of his female characters—queen or princess —say,

> " Why are our bodies soft, and weak, and smooth ;
> Unapt to toil and trouble in the world ?
> But that our soft conditions and our hearts
> Should well agree with our external parts."

Again, there are many things of less or more importance which come to require a single ultimate decision. *One* must say how this thing is to be. Of course, if there be agreement on the matter, there can be no difficulty. But say there is *not* agreement, that the judgment of husband and wife are diverse the one from the other : from no wilfulness on the part of either ; and connected with no passion or temper of any kind or degree. It is a simple honest difference of opinion. Practical action *must* be taken one way or other. Who shall decide ? Is the husband to submit to the wife ? No one will say so unless with reference to a few cases.

The utmost that would be contended for would be some kind of joint-authority. But we are supposing a case in which it does not work, and cannot work. Neither is to blame. Neither has any improper feeling towards the other ; a joint-judgment cannot be reached,—and yet action must be taken. How? would not every true-minded woman feel in such a case—" I am glad that my husband must decide ? With that decision, aided as it is by the knowledge of my opinion, and after a full consideration of it, I shall gladly fall in. After all there is agreement—for that to me is in such a case the will of God. *He* decides with whom God has lodged the responsibility."

But the truth is that in a properly regulated, or rather a properly inspired home, the question of authority in its bald form never arises. The husband's rule and the wife's obedience are alike unconscious, and alike easy. The sweet laws of nature, the good laws of God, make them one.

But what about the homes that are *not* properly regulated ? What about the authority of the husband when it is stretched until it becomes oppression, or—put in this con-

crete case—what about the behaviour of
Vashti ? · Was she right or wrong ?

This leads us to say, on the other hand,
with equal emphasis, that the authority of the
husband *is clearly a limited authority*. Common sense ought to teach a man that there
is a large sphere of the practical family life
where he ought to leave the wife and mother
practically supreme. His interference at all
(whatever may be the abstract right) will
not help the industry, the order, the peace of
the household.

But, rising higher, look at the grand fact
that the authority of the husband over the
wife has, and must have, clear and strong,
and altogether impassable limits. She is a
complete human being. She has all the
moral responsibilities of any other human
creature—man or woman. She has her own
conscience ; her own will ; her own heart ;
her own soul. She stands in the grand
relations ; is under the unchallengeable and
unchangeable law of God ; is bound to render
obedience *to Him* against whatever opposition,
at whatever cost. The authority of the husband, or any other human authority, is nothing

here.   She may say as Peter and John did to
the Jewish rulers when they wished them to
render absolute submission and hold their
peace,—" Whether it be right in the sight of
God to hearken unto you more than unto
God judge ye."   She will say it in such a
case as gently as it can be said, and so as to
gain her liberty of action, if it may be so,
without a struggle.   But say it she must, and
will.   Any one consciously untrue to God
and disobedient to the highest law cannot be
deeply true in the lower relations.   In fact
it comes to this, that only the wife who
serves God in spirit *can* truly serve her husband.   A craven submission is not the loyal
loving obedience spoken of in the Scriptures.
Still there remains the point where the pinch
is, and the line where the shadow lies, and
where there is the flitting uncertainty.   A true-
minded woman will be always duly disposed to
self-jealousy and self-interrogation.   She will
say, " Am I *quite* sure that God requires this
of me ?   Am I not gently smuggling in self-
will, and calling it will of God ?   Might I not
in this give up my own way, and follow my
husband's, and find it the way of God ?"   Just

as a true-minded husband will say, "Am I right in requiring this when I see that the rendering of it costs my wife a struggle?" There are a hundred questions in practical life which only love can answer; a hundred difficulties which only love can solve.

Then, was Vashti right or wrong in her refusal to come at the king's commandment? You must just give your own answer, for we have no authoritative teaching on the subject. If you care to have our opinion, here it is:— We think, or feel more than think, that she was quite right, and highly to be praised. The mandate *did* transgress the limit. It was a mandate which neither husband nor king had any right to issue. It touched her purity, her womanhood, her intuitional queenliness, and she trampled it in the dust. The act was brave in whatever spirit it was done. If she did it with any view of the possible consequence, and knowing that she might thereby lose her crown, it was noble! Indeed her mien and deportment, as she passes thus swiftly across the stage before us, is queenly and majestic. She is one of two illustrious women celebrated in this book, and, to our

mind, she is rather the better of the two.   We
know very little of the real inner character of
either of them ; but as far as we do know, or
may conjecture, Vashti is nobler than Esther.

The chamberlains hasten back to the king
in surprise and dismay, and give in the fateful
answer.   Of course the great monarch, already
inflamed with wine, easily burns with rage.
Probably in the whole course of his reign no
slight like this has come to him.   Think of
it.   The banquet at its height of splendour !
The princes from far and near around him !
The whisper has gone round, " She is coming
—the peerless one with the crown royal
upon her head, and the highest beauty of the
earth   upon   her   face." . . . Then,   in   a
moment, blackness is seen to gather on the
monarch's face, and the whisper goes round
yet faster, " She is *not* coming.   She has refused to come."

Of course the matter could not so end.
But the king's rage did not break out into any
wild and senseless ebullition.   The refusal,
while it angered, seems also to have sobered
him.   He never thought of using physical
force—as compelling the queen into confine-

ment.   Our English King Henry would have probably made shorter work with any English queen in the like case.   Ahasuerus at once resolves that the matter shall be settled according to the ancient laws of the Empire, and with this end he avails himself of the judgment of the wise men, the lawyers, and the statesmen of his court.   They were also " princes "—those who, not only by rank, but because of their proved wisdom and experi- ence,—stood nearest to him—those " who saw his face."   The Persian and Median monarchs lived in a privacy which was sacred and inviolable.   His great minister—charged with the affairs of Empire—saw him ; but, on ordinary occasions, few besides.

Of course in an emergency like this they are earnestly consulted.   And they are not long in giving the answer.   Apparently they have no difficulty.   They decide at once, and Memucan, the leader — the Prince Prime Minister—speaks for the rest, before the king and the princes, and tells how they are all agreed, not only that Vashti has done wrong to the king, but to all the princes, and to all the husbands in Persia.   The recusant queen had struck a blow which would be felt, and might be repeated in every house in the land. They seem to have been afraid of a social insurrection. " The ladies of Persia and Media," they say, " will all rebel against their lords, and plead the queen's example !" And perhaps the wise men were right. It would not have been safe to pass such a matter over. " Too much contempt and wrath,"—contempt in the women, and wrath in the men,—would have been spread immediately through the land. Ah! but the king should have thought of all this before ; as we should all think more than we do, before we act. And, especially where acts are doubtful, yet *must* have long consequences. One wrong act seldom or never stands alone—like a pillar on a plain. It necessitates other wrong acts to follow. The queen is right, and yet she must be punished, because, more evil (in the judgment of these men which we are in no condition to contest), more evil would come to the state and society by granting her impunity than any that could come to her personally by the possible hardship involved in her sentence of deposition. That is the sentence they pronounce, as far as they have the power to do so—" Let her be deposed. Let her see the king's face no more. Let the crown pass to another : and the royal estate—the palaces and the pageantry— unto another that is better than she." And the thing was done. The king was pleased. The decree was passed in due and solemn form. And it was published far and wide, by letters sent into all the provinces, and written in the several languages of the various tribes and peoples, written out duly by the scribes and linguists of their foreign office ; and this was the substance of the decree :— " That every man should bear rule in his own house :" and this its object :—" That all the wives should give to their husbands honour, both to great and small."

The forecast thus made by these wise men of the result throughout the great empire of the publication of the decree, is probably on the whole a correct one. Our phrase for such a decree would be " statesmanlike." And yet it is almost impossible to read the terms of it without some rising of amused feeling; without some emotion of scorn. *All*

the husbands are embraced in it ; and it provides that they are all to share alike. All
the *wives* too are included, for they are all
" to give honour to their husbands, both to
the great and *small.*" Well, the great, the
really great, will get the honour easily, and
could do very well probably without the
helpful edict. Where there is real greatness,
which, in Christian speech, we may trans-
late into real *goodness*, it is the wife's joy to
render what it is the husband's pride to wear.
But the honour is to be given " both to the
great and *small !*" " Ay, there's the rub."
If this insurrectionary torch should go
through the land, what will become of the
small ones ? — the selfish, the spiteful, the
meddlesome, the rude, the mean, the silly,
the helpless, the good-for-nothing ? They
are *all* to have honour ! As if a decree could
really get it, or keep it for them. Wouldn't
the better plan be, in that case, and in many
a case besides, that the small shall try to
grow larger ? Let them be ashamed of their
littleness, and rise out of it into something
like nobleness. Let them love and help
their wives, and care for their children, and

think of others : and stir themselves up to exertion and manly ways—and then the honour will come as harvest follows sowing. But unless they do something like that, one fears that all the edicts that can be devised and promulgated will leave them as it finds them—" small."

So they parted. It was a literal and life-long severance, accomplished, probably, not without private sorrows and relentings each towards the other ; perhaps not without sighs and tears. The first verse of the next chapter tells us that " the king remembered Vashti,"—it is a little touch of nature and tenderness which makes us think more kindly of the great monarch. And we may be sure that Vashti remembered the king ! and earnestly wished that things could have been otherwise; and blamed those rude and odious princes, through whose means she would be ready to think the thing had come about— but so it was. They parted to meet no more. It is an old story: and yet, alas ! ever new. It does not need king and queen to make a touching tragedy like this. It can be acted in very humble circumstances.

Hands joined at the marriage - altar are pulled asunder. Hearts which have throbbed to each other in mutual love and sympathy are cooled and severed ; or, sadder yet, are severed without being much cooled. The drunkenness of a night, leading, it may be, to something worse, or the fierce gust of passion suddenly aroused, or some mood of dull unchallenged selfishness, or some bitter, thoughtless words, or some headstrong ways on the part of either, or both, and it is done,—kingly honour sits no more on the husband's head to the wife's view ; the crown-royal is worn no longer by the wife, as the husband sees her, and then they part, to meet no more.

> " They parted, ne'er to meet again,
>   But never either found another
>   To free the hollow heart from paining ;
>   They stood aloof, the scars remaining,
>   Like cliffs which had been rent asunder ;
>   A dreary sea now flows between,
>   But neither heat, nor frost, nor thunder,
>   Shall wholly do away, I ween,
>   The marks of that which once hath been."

Far other than this is the picture we are to look at and realise for ourselves, standing

in one or other of the great relations compre-
hended in that word "home." There is a
divine wisdom given to men who seek it for
daily guidance through this ever-changing, and
sometimes very perplexing human life. Those
who in all their ways acknowledge God *have*
the fulfilment of His promise that " He will
direct their paths." There is a love which
can hold human hearts together, even when
all things seek to pull them apart—a love
which surmounts reverses, which softens
hardship, which makes poverty not indeed
desirable, but endurable, which lives on
through the changes of a fickle world, and is
immortalised by death. As husbands and
wives, as parents and children, as brothers
and sisters, we have but to realise and
accomplish what is meant by that word
" Home !" and we shall do well. True in
these relations,

"Onward we have but to press,
   Through the paths of duty ;
Virtue is true happiness,
   Excellence true beauty.
Love is of celestial birth,
   Make we then a heaven of earth.

"Closer, closer, let us knit
   Hearts and hands together,
Where our fireside comforts sit
   In the wildest weather.
O ! they wander wide who roam
   For the joys of life from Home."

LECTURE III.

CHAPTER II., i. to xx.

THE NEW QUEEN.

"AFTER these things"—the things narrated in the first chapter. It must have been a considerable time after. In the third year of his reign was the great feast held which had such an unlooked-for termination. And it was not until the seventh year of his reign, at the end of the year (v. 16), that the queenly throne was filled by Vashti's successor. How is this delay to be accounted for? What was the king doing? Is it not very unlikely that one so violent in his passions would wait so long? Those who believe that Ahasuerus is Xerxes (which is, we think, the true supposition) can account for those years fully, by the monarch's movements and by great historical events. It is known that Xerxes was absent from Persia in his fourth year. He passed the winter of that year in Sardis. He set forward thence in the spring of the year following.

The battle of Thermopylæ was fought in the summer, and that of Salamis in the autumn ; and in the year after that, took place the battles of Platæa and Mycale. Then he returned to Sardis—and thence, in a while, to Susa. Thus the four years are pretty well accounted for. They were years of disaster, and (perhaps somewhat in consequence of this) of dissolute living. For misfortune and reverse have the same kind of effects upon monarchs that they have upon other men. Some they humble and improve, and some they exasperate and harden.

Yet this vanquished soldier, this disgraced and dissolute man, is still monarch of Persia! And the more he has failed abroad, the more he must succeed at home, if he is to keep his throne. " Let everything then," he seems to have said, "go on in the full style of splendour. Let no glory die—and the queen—I must have a queen ! "

E

It is said the king's servants suggested this to him. But kings' servants know pretty well what to suggest. No doubt, however, the policy of having another queen-royal had the approbation of the wise men, else it could not have been carried out successfully.

And then began the preparation, the narrative of which needs no illustration of ours. It is perfectly plain : and it is not edifying. And yet *it is*. Rightly read—under due emotions and reflections, it *is* edifying (and especially to the female part of the world), in the highest degree. That *ought* to be edifying which shows much cause for gratitude. Now just look at that picture of Persian female life of the highest kind. Persia —the mistress of civilisation at the time: the seat of wealth and splendour : the land of the brave and the wise. And this is how it treats its noblest women ! Could female degradation be more complete ? All the more complete that none wondered: none protested: none resisted—unless we may take Vashti's rebellion as a kind of moral insurrection against the whole treatment and state of woman. If it was so, it spent itself. For

here they come from far and near—the
young, the fair, the nobly-born—as well as
those of humbler condition in their miserable
darkness, thinking that an honour (without a
thought of wrong about it), which would now
be esteemed, in any Christian country, the
deepest disgrace. To use the words of an
English bishop on this chapter, " It is," he
says, " of priceless worth, as showing the need
under which the human race then lay, of
that deliverance which has been wrought by
the incarnation of the Son of God, the seed
of the woman, who raised womanhood to a
high and holy dignity, and by that spiritual
espousal of a church universal, by which he
has sanctified marriage, and made it a great
mystery. And it may remind the world of
the inestimable benefits it owes to Christianity." Also, one ought to say, that the
narrative of this chapter, although we pass it
over lightly, is quite purely written. Now
this matter ought to be faced, plainly.
Sceptics and enemies of the faith are in the
habit of alleging or insinuating that there are
not a few passages in Holy Writ not fit to
be read in families and congregations—

hardly in closets. A considerable number of
passages certainly are not *suitable* for public
reading or exposition. Therefore they are
not read ; and they are not expounded,
except for some special ends. But impure
passages, indelicate corrupting passages ?
Not one. The breath of God has passed
through this chapter, and it is clear and
clean, so that no one of simple mind will get
harm by reading it. Would any one say the
same regarding some of our fashionable
novels and tales ?——many of them, softly be
it spoken, and sorrowfully, and with shame,
written by women ! ! — by women calling
themselves Christians, who, at any rate, have
received the benefit of the Christian civilisation so far, who therefore have been elevated
—away beyond heathen female life. And
this is the way they behave themselves, and
show their gratitude. They spend their
energies and their genius, such as it is, in
corrupting their fellow-creatures, filling the
minds of the young with evil suggestions,
which either distress them, or pollute and
deprave them : working up disgusting situations, and horrible scenes ; making light of

the holiest ties of human life, and apologising for some of its deepest evils and crimes.

I am not speaking at random, although I do not profess to be speaking from any extensive personal knowledge ; because I for one will not, and do not read such books, if I know it —not as fearing any great personal harm, for one may hope that one's disgust would always be too great to make any harm possible ; but it does one harm to be even disgusted unnecessarily. On reliable authority, by consensus of judgment of the most impartial description, I believe this matter needs the attention of good people far more urgently than some other things which secure that attention. At any rate, I feel quite sure that I am but doing my duty in thus testifying and warning. One thing we can all do, we can refuse to read. Happily there is enough *good* literature of every kind—not heavy, dull, solemn, but fresh, bright, humorous, pathetic, comic, tragic —all kinds of the really good, by writers both alive and dead. So that there is no excuse for going down into the slough ; " Keep thyself pure."

But it is time to go on with our story.

New characters now come on the stage; especially the two principal characters of the book, and we may almost say of the generation in which they lived — Mordecai and Esther. Neither of them of any note at the time they begin to act, but both of them, as the sequel shows, highly capable of making history, and acting worthily in the most conspicuous situations. In fact, the character of both the one and the other is quite a study. They are colourless people when we first see them; and although they become more pronounced as the drama unfolds itself, they never stand out, morally and religiously, among the best. There is material in the narrative for forming a very favourable judgment of both of them; and there is also some material for forming almost an adverse judgment. The conclusion one comes to is, that we had better not confidently judge them either the one way or the other, although there is, I think, enough to justify a highly favourable judgment, but regard them as chosen actors and instruments in the hands of Providence in a critical time, rather than as prepared and sanctified specimens of goodness.

Mordecai is introduced to us as "*a certain Jew*" living in Shushan the Palace. Any one having prepossession *against* Mordecai can say—"What was he doing there at all ? A man of energy and capacity, why had he not returned to Jerusalem *with* those, or *after* them, who had been set free ? Patriotism would have carried him to Palestine : condemns him living still in Persia." But this is to take a very narrow view of the case. Remember it was this man's grandfather or great-grandfather who had been carried captive into Babylon. *He* had been born in the captivity, and brought up among the people and amid the customs of the place ; and he may have seen (there is some reason for supposing that he did) that the best service he could render to his people and country could be rendered in Shushan and not in Jerusalem.

In the house with him is a Jewish girl, Hadassah, really a cousin of his own, for she was his uncle's daughter, but so much younger than himself that he has adopted her as a daughter, and is bringing her up in the nurture and admonition of his people. Father and mother both gone—what a loss ! Poor little orphan girl! The world will be hard and cold to her now. But she would be told of one who is "the Father of the fatherless;" and surely never any one had more occasion to say, "When my father and mother forsake me, then the Lord will take me up."

And yet also do not you see in Esther *something* which almost tells of the lack of a mother's tenderness and care in her earliest years; a certain clear, passionless, almost masculine strength of purpose, but not softened with any flushing of emotion. However, she is now a girl in her loving protector's house; she is his child. He is evidently a man of high capacity, fit for affairs of state as soon as they come into his hands, and she is, of course, educated in the best manner. She never could have been Queen of Persia without high accomplishments. She was also "fair and beautiful," or "*fair of form and good of countenance.*" Evidently she possessed unusual beauty. Her Hebrew maiden name was Hadassah—myrtle; her Persian queenly name was Esther—star.

One of the great difficulties of the Book is the difficulty of understanding how

Mordecai *could* think of entering his ward, his adopted child, on such a competition at all. There was no difficulty to any Persian family —they were but falling in with the ancient custom. Political movements were often advanced in connection with these royal alliances, just as they are at this day in all the European countries, although now in a less degree than formerly. But Mordecai is a Jew—a strict Jew in many things, a real lover of his country and people ; and it *is* matter of wonder that he can venture a Jewish maiden, one to whom he is tenderly attached—his very child of adoption, into such a sea of dread uncertainty. Some think that he must have had divine intimation either expressly communicated, or rising strongly in his own convictions as to the issue of the trial. When the parents of Moses " saw that he was a proper child they hid him three months." Something, as it were, told them instinctively that this child was to be the deliverer of his people. In like manner Mordecai *may* have had it impressed upon his mind irresistibly that this child (as dear as she was fair) would be the instrument for great benefits to her people. But this is simply a kindly conjecture, and there really is no historical foundation for it. We are always in danger of regarding a course of human action in the light of its results. If those results are highly favourable, and if the divine hand has been conspicuously displayed in bringing them about, the means employed to bring them are apt to pass with much less than the usual criticism. Indeed, it is apt to seem almost like a presumptuous human judgment on divine providence itself if we venture to say " This and this was wrong "! " Wrong? how can it be, when God has deigned to use it as his own instrumentality for working his holy and perfect will?" So we mingle and confuse things which are perfectly and for ever apart. The moral merit, or demerit, of what I do is one thing. God's *use* of what I do, and his applications of it to the promotion of his own good ends—that is quite another thing. What we do is right or wrong in itself,—or it is partly right and partly wrong,—and it is for the moral character of the action that we are answerable. The consequences (owing, it may be, to a great many other things) may be disastrous—we are not responsible for that, or (owing again to a great many other things) they may be most excellent—we have no merit in that. The merit and demerit lie in the action, not in any concomitants or consequents.

The same principle is to be applied in our judgments of the conduct of others,—in so far as we judge them. We are not to judge our neighbours in an evil uncharitable sense. But we are to judge our neighbours in a broad, and candid, and fair manner. Still more ought we to make fair judgment regarding our predecessors, whose names and deeds are on the page of history. Their lives will be of little use to us unless we do.

It is particularly necessary to judge the Scripture characters of all kinds, and the particular acts of the men and women *in themselves considered*, and not merely in the light of their historic effects. We are not to ask regarding any one—Mordecai or Esther, or any one else, " Is this man, this woman, a saint or a sinner ? and then explain everything in the light of the answer we get, or

give. Rather, we are to take the actions, one
by one, or the course of action, and in the
light of the great moral principles of the
Scriptures, which never change, which are as
inflexible as the divine nature itself, we are
humbly to form and express our estimates—
" This is wrong, no matter what comes of it !
This is right, no matter what comes of it !"

Well, judged in this way, what are we to
say regarding the conduct of Mordecai, in
sending his child into this great national
competition for a jaded monarch's heart—or
rather for the supreme place and power in
the kingdom next to that of the monarch ?
No doubt there are many things to be taken
into account, some of them perhaps quite unknown to us. But we confess we do not see
how he *could* be justified in any view of the
case that can be taken. He was a Jew, and
well instructed. He had, *i.e.* he knew, the pure
religion—the pure morals. He knew what
was right and the will of God ; and he ought
not to have sent that girl—young, fair, artless,
and, as far as appears through the whole
history, perfectly simple and pure—up into
the king's Harem to take the chances. It

was a success—but suppose it had been a
failure ? Then he has sacrificed the child.
He has lost her even for himself, and with
her the objects of his ambition or of his
patriotism.

Just *such* risks are run, although of course
not amid circumstances so conspicuous and
splendid, by those who promote alliances for
their children with supreme or exclusive
regard to wealth, station, and other outward
things. If moral character be not regarded,
be not required in the man sought or accepted
for a husband to the child or the ward—if it
be chiefly what he has, and where he stands
in the social scale—well, the marriage may
turn out happily enough, for men are often
better than they are known to be until they
are tried ; but sometimes also they are worse,
and then ?—yes, sometimes *greatly* worse, and
then ?—the married life is a ghastly awakening, a long-drawn and still-increasing pain.
The man's love was but a whim. It is soon
over. He is selfish, slippery, carnal, untrue.
He seeks enjoyment chiefly in the satisfaction
of his passions. He tramples roughly on the
tenderest affections. And there are tears

shed in secret by her who trusted and has been thus grievously disappointed. And touches of pain may be seen on her countenance ; and her secret life is a sigh. Can *any* outward advantages compensate for this? and when this comes, as it does sometimes, together with a complete collapse of those very advantages——the misery is complete.

"Mordecai walked every day before the court of the women's house, to know how Esther did, and what should become of her." And it is probable that on some particular days his reflections were not very enviable. Ah! how many a house has been thus watched since then? How many are watched now? by those who, in heart, and sometimes even literally, like Mordecai, walk up and down, waiting to hear some tidings of the caged and suffering creature within.

Our Esthers take the matter of their own life-alliance more into their own hands, as it is right they should. To *them*, therefore, as well as to the Mordecais——the fathers, the mothers, the uncles, the guardians, — this warning word should come. Seek first to find the true and loving heart in him, in her, to whom you give your hand. Seek first a companionship that will be helpful and ennobling to you whatever the outward fortunes may be, and all other things will be added. After all we must trust each other in a large measure. We cannot know everything beforehand. Young people cannot know each other. They do not know even themselves. They do not know, therefore, what kind of husbands and wives they will make to each other. Go on cheerfully then on probabilities. But let them be probabilities looking the right way, not the wrong way, and then be hopeful of all good. So it be the true Esther, whether she be on the throne, or in the little house of the quiet street, doesn't so much matter. There is a " star "-like beauty which will shine above all outward splendours, and which no obscurity can quench. It is " the beauty of the Lord our God upon " his faithful people, and those who shine in it are Daniels and Esthers wherever they may be. (And if not married, never mind.)

Well—we all know the issue of the trial. The monarch declares himself captivated—

really is so, for he had no motive to say anything but the truth in the case, with the charms of the Jewish maiden (not knowing her to be so as yet).   Now this means, we cannot help thinking, far more than we usually comprehend in the term "beauty." It means a high order of accomplishment in Esther.   As the monarch thought, and as the sequel proved, she was every inch a queen.

In due time she is so proclaimed.   And *the feast* is held, without which nothing grand can be accomplished—modern London is like ancient Persia in this.   It was *Esther's* feast ; and it was great.   There was release in the provinces, and bountiful giving, and universal joy.   And Mordecai walks no more in the court, waiting for tidings with an anxious heart.   And his faith is rewarded, if what he did was done in faith.   And in any case his political views are advanced, and he is one step—one *great* step, nearer the position where he will be able to protect his people from some terrible storms that seem gathering.   And, above all, the providence of God is seen in the very process of one of its most

wonderful achievements ; and seen, not the
less illustriously, because there is so much
that may be exceptionable in the human
action of the individuals concerned.   We do
not need to justify Mordecai in everything ;
or Esther in everything ; or, still more, the
king in his universal lawlessness, in order to
see the working of a perfect providence in all.

The individual agents do their will, and
take their way as they can—some striving for
this, and some for that—and the will and the
way of God come out of them serenely, perfectly !   But do not you see what a wonderful
chain of events it is, out of which the ultimate
providential purpose is evolved, and how a failure or a change anywhere—in what we call a
little thing—would alter the whole effect ?
Say that the feast had been interrupted, even
on its last day, before the king's heart was
merry with wine—nothing would then have
happened of all this history.   Say that the
vain thought of exhibiting his queen had
never entered into his mind—nothing would
have happened.   Say that Vashti had come
when she was sent for—again nothing would
have happened.   Say that Esther's father and

mother had not died—she would have been at home with them, and *they* would not have thought of doing as Mordecai did. And so on through a great number of possible suppositions. A link dropped in a chain spoils the chain. It will pull nothing, hold nothing. Any *one* event of a long series dropped out would alter all that comes after. God's providence, therefore, is minute and particular. It concerns all that happens—all that men think, and do, and are. Human freedom is untouched, and yet divine will is perfectly wrought ; and if only we are on the side of that divine will as far as we know it, submitting and conforming our own will to the will of God, then we may be entirely sure that providence is on our side. The smallest things in our life are the objects of divine regard. The hairs of our head are all numbered, our tears are kept by God as men keep the choicest wines, our sighs are heard, our steps directed, our " goings out " and our " comings in " preserved from that time forth, when we give ourselves truly to Him, on through life to its ending, and even for evermore.

If, on the other hand, we are governed by

self-will, having no respect for the will of God, except in so far as it may seem to chime in with our own, we may be as entirely sure that providence is against us—at any rate, can never be " for us"—while we continue in such a state of mind. It might set a crown upon our head, put a kingdom into our hands, lay our name on the four winds, to be borne wherever breezes whisper or waters murmur in human ears, yet all the while in its secret spirit, and in the full weight of its eternal force, it would be against us. And if we die in that state, settled in self-will, what will happen? Just this : the providence of the world into which we go will be against us, exactly as was the providence of this world when we left it ; and if a man could die, or fly if you will, out of one world into another, and then into another continually and eternally, he would never find a world the providence of which would be for him, unless there be another God. Everything, then, you see depends on having the humble, obedient, holy will. Our inner state will rule for us all outer things. " He that doeth the will of God abideth for ever."

True, it is a very great matter; indeed it is *everything* to get this renewed will. And to some it may seem impossible. "We are what we are, and such we must remain; we can only develop, we cannot change." But the gospel says, "No; there is no such necessity. With God all things are possible. The gospel is forgiveness; the gospel is regeneracy; the gospel is power; the gospel is the breath of God in the soul of man. As on some trees the leaves hang long—through the autumn, through the dark, dripping winter, scar and sapless and sooty, and yet will not fall off and die, although shaken by many a blast, but fall off quite easily on some early spring day when not a breath is stirring without, because the irresistible force of new life is stirring within—so when a man is in Christ he is a new creature, and when he is a new creature old things naturally and easily pass away, and all things become new."

LECTURE IV.

CHAPTER III.

HAMAN AND MORDECAI.

ORDECAI is "sitting in the king's gate." Some call him a humble porter, or gate-opener, getting thus the effect of contrast between the humble position and the great service he was able to render in a particular case in protecting and preserving the monarch. But this is a mistake. To stand or sit in the gate was to be near the person of the king, and to be high in office. No position is contemptible in itself. But a man of Mordecai's gifts and capacities was not likely to be found in the lowest kind of service; he is in the king's gate, and of course in official association with many more—chamberlains and ministers of state.

Some way or other, we are not told how, he becomes aware of the existence of a treasonable plot against the king's life. He may have been consulted by the traitors ; or hints may have been dropped in his hearing to see if he would take them up ; or, without becoming an eavesdropper, he may have overheard some whisperings of evil omen ; or, suspecting something amiss, he *may* have become an eavesdropper. Some way or other, "the thing became known" to him ; and he lost no time in making it known to the king, through Esther, the queen. The thing was soon fully discovered and laid open, and the conspirators—Bigthana and Teresh—were "hanged on a tree" (*i.e.* crucified), and the thing was written in the Book of the Chronicles before the king. A true picture of Persian court-life ! If any one asks farther proof of the probability of such a thing, it is at hand in the unquestioned historic fact that Xerxes "was actually murdered, at night in his bed, by two persons, one of whom was a chamberlain and the other a chief captain of his

guard." The thing was of frequent occur-
rence in Persian history ; indeed we may say
that this kind of thing has been a constant
and ghastly attendant on despotic rule in
every country. When any one is endowed
with irresponsible power ; when the lives of
others are in his hands ; when all things and
all persons, great and small, are made to bend
to his convenience and contribute to his glory ;
when he withholds his heart from no joy, he
is not the happier, and certainly he is not the
safer by all this, but only by so much the
more exposed. Some request denied, some
courtier's mortified ambition, or some ill-
regulated impulse of true patriotism ; or some
brooding injury that has come of the monarch's
lawless indulgence ; or some capricious mood
of which no account could be given—any of
these things, or things less still than these,
can shape the arrow or sharpen the sword
that will drink the heart's blood of a king.

The same law runs through universal life.
High station, anywhere in the social scale,
does not of itself bring either contentment or
safety. The sleepless pillow is seldom the
hardest ; is often the downiest. The house

that has most of "home" in it, in the deepest
and dearest sense of the word, is seldom the
house with the greatest number of rooms in
it : is far more often the house where a little
pressure is now and then needed, and always
a good deal of motherly and sisterly skill in
getting everything into daily fettle and trim.
In lowliness is safety. Labour, unless it be
over-work, sweetens pleasure. The old lesson
meets us at every turn — "Neither poverty
nor riches." If we were poor, we should be
sure to steal, if not with our fingers, with our
thoughts — with our hunger, our envy, our
hankering cares ; and if we were rich, God
knows! we might forget Him, and go strut-
ting about as masters when, in fact, we are
only tenants and hired servants, holding our
life-farm by the day. We who are of the
middle ranks ought to be, as far as our condition is concerned, among the safest and
happiest of mankind. If there be truth in
this book, and if we are not mere pretenders
to faith in it, then "the lines have fallen unto
us in pleasant places, and we have a goodly
heritage."

But now there comes suddenly upon the

stage, like a Macbeth or a Richard the Third, one of the great characters of this book, Haman. The name is supposed to signify The Illustrious. Famous he has certainly made himself through all time. His name and deeds will live as long as those of Esther. He was an Agagite, a descendant of the Amalekite kings. Amalek laid wait for Israel when he came up out of Egypt, and fought against him in Rephidim. His cruelty was gratuitous and malicious in a high degree ; and for great moral and public reasons it was never to be forgiven. Amalek was to be destroyed. Saul had the opportunity of doing it, failed to do it, and lost his crown.

Here is Haman in Persia : Prime Minister of the great empire ; an able, unscrupulous man ; a man of the loftiest pride ; of boundless ambition ; a very good representative of the bitter and malignant nation from whose kings he has come. And his port is kingly. He knows how to exact homage, how to smile and frown, how to win and terrify. He rides forth to-day from the king's presence, bearing with him the king's commandment for all he may require. See how the courtiers make obeisance, and how the people prostrate themselves in the dust while he passes by! But there is one who will not fall down, who will not even rise from his seat. He is not blind ; he sees the coming pomp. He is not deaf; he hears the murmurs of adulation, but still he moves not. " Oh, the man is a foreigner, and does not understand. Let him be told of the king's commandment, and then he'll bow like the rest." He is told, and still does not bow. He is remonstrated with, and counselled to do according to the royal behest, but in vain. Haman may come and go, but he shall get no more notice from Mordecai than the humblest menial of the palace. Why? Has he a reason? Yes; he is a Jew. " He told them that he was a Jew," and as such could not render to man the reverence which was due only to God, *and* to those (the king and the priest) who were personally and expressly God's ministers and representatives. But it is more than probable that other reasons were working in his heart. One cannot but think that some method of testifying respect to the king's representative, which would have done no violence to his

conscience, and which would have got him
through, might have been found if he had
been anxious to find it.   But the old national
antipathy is strong within him, and has its
counterpart in equal strength in the breast of
Haman.   This meeting of Jew and Agagite
is the meeting of fire and water.   One must
be consumed.   There is probably an instinct
in the heart of Mordecai that peace is impossible, and that even safety for himself and
his people is not to be attained under the
supremacy of this man.

At any rate the conflict is begun.   You see
a man may begin a deadly quarrel by simply
sitting still and keeping silence.   The world
says, " Shout, for I am coming !"   The world
says, " Fall upon your face, for I am passing
by !"   And if he does not do it, the world
will say, " He is disloyal, that he is fanatical,
that he is setting himself above the law."
Thus the law is inflexible, perpetual.   The
friend of the world is the enemy of God.
Observe, this is not fanciful moralising.   It
is the lesson (one of the lessons) of the passage.   " Amalek is a scriptural type of Satan
and his powers, the spiritual enemy of God

and his people." Only in this way can we fully understand, or perhaps fully justify, such a word as this, *e.g.* (Deuteronomy xxv. 17), " Remember what Amalek did unto thee by the way, when ye were come forth out of Egypt ; how he met thee by the way and smote the hindmost of thee, even all that were feeble behind thee, when thou wast faint and weary ; *and he feared not God.*" Isn't that the devil's way always — to smite the hindmost, the feeblest, the weariest ? To watch for the pilgrim's halting ? To strike at the soldier when his armour is off ? And has the world any mercy ? or will it ever have ? War with Amalek from generation to generation, until his remembrance is blotted out from under heaven. No bowing down to Haman, whatever his splendour, whatever his power. Even as Christ, from the devil on the mountain-top having the offer of all the kingdoms of the world, and the glory of them, on the single condition of falling down and worshipping Haman's chief, said, " Get thee hence, Satan ; Thou shalt worship the Lord thy God, and Him only shalt thou serve."

The matter, of course, soon came to Haman's knowledge. There were plenty to tell him. As far as the narrative tells us, they seem to have been actuated by no improper motive. It was their duty to see that the law was observed and the commandment of the king obeyed. But possibly some among them were willing enough to tell Haman of Mordecai's recusancy. Possibly enough they did not much like this clever, watching, pushing Jew, and were not ill-pleased with the prospect of his having a fall, and being taken out of the way of their own advancement.

And now the eyes of the great minister as he passes out of the gate are turned full on Mordecai, and his face flushes with rage and hatred. But it isn't a personal contest with this solitary man that he will wage. He feels, perhaps, that he could have him hung to-morrow if he were to set his heart on it. But—"they had showed him the *people of Mordecai*"—the Jews scattered through the city and through all the cities. "Ha!" he seems to have said with himself, "I know them, as my fathers knew them. They are our hereditary foes. They will make no peace with us, and as long as the blood of the royal house of Amalek flows in my veins I shall make no peace with them. We shall see which nation is first 'blotted out from under heaven!' I hate them, with their industry, and their greed, and their intoler- ance. My great revenge has stomach for them all!" " He thought scorn to lay hands on Mordecai *alone*, for they had showed him the people of Mordecai."

To manage the king in the matter was easy. He was not moving up and down among his people. He dwelt in absolute seclusion, and was dependent on his ministers for information ; and here is one who has proved himself to be jealous of the king's honour, and zealous for the good of the empire. What *he* counsels will be best. And so the thing is arranged, and the edict for the destruction of these disloyal plotting Jews is virtually taken. But it must be executed in due form—legally, religiously. The lot must be cast to see at what time the gods ordain the massacre ("the lot is cast into the lap, but the whole disposing thereof is of the Lord "). It was cast many times, and with all due solemnities, in the *first* month of the year, but the omens would not settle on any nearer time for action than the *last* month of the year. Haman would have hailed the second month, or the third, with joy, feeling, no doubt, that " If 'twere well done, 'twere well it were done quickly." And the king's treasuries would be the sooner enriched with the promised spoil of the doomed people. We see from this that they had settled in the country, entered upon trade, amassed wealth —for this strange people have always been a money-making race, largely, probably, because they have not been allowed to hold other property. It is singular, and not without significance in relation to the future, that at this hour, and through the whole realm of civilisation, more than any other people, and much beyond the proportion which their numbers would allow, they touch the springs of monetary action, actually hold the money of the nations, and, by its means, influence largely the daily and monthly literature of Europe, especially the political literature.

Such, then, is the situation—an unprincipled monarch willing to do anything, however inhuman, to purchase safety, and indulgence in every favourite pleasure. A cruel, crafty, ambitious, grand vizier with an old grudge to settle, as well as present designs to advance—holding in his hands, for the time, absolute power, and the sign and shield of it in the possession of the king's ring. What chance has this poor scattered people— a few here, a few there, with no organisation, no weapons of war, no leader, no military courage, no political ability—against odds so overwhelming as these? *This* chance, that there is in the heavens a hater of wrong, a helper of the helpless, a divine controller of *all* that happens on the earth—One who exercises that control alike by the march of irresistible armies, and by the apparently capricious movements of the signs, whatever they were, of the lot falling before the eyes of the king. Every month is tried, and only the *last* month is suitable. "On the last month then let it be," says grim Haman. "'Tis long to wait, but the work may be the more surely done. None, in the farthest provinces, or in the most obscure condition, shall now escape."

And anon the scribes are busy. The deadly edict is written out in many languages, and sent to the rulers of all the several peoples composing the great nation, signed, and sealed with the king's ring. And soon the posts are on the road, hastened by the king's commandment. And the two chief authors and agents of this devilish decree—are they troubled ? Have they compunctious visitings ? Do they think of the mothers, of the little children, who will perish in their homes or on the streets ? We cannot know all their thoughts. It is quite possible that they had some strong relentings. But there was no hesitation in their action : and, as far as the narrative goes, there was none in their feeling. With a sense of relief apparently, and breathing more freely, as though they had escaped some great danger, " the king and Haman sat down to drink," while " the city Shushan was perplexed." Or, if there were touches of remorse and natural sorrow, or any gigantic shadows of coming danger rising on them out of the horrors which they had just ordained, all such perturbations and apprehensions will best be allayed in the deep

G

wine-cup.   O wine, thou consoler! thou
deceiver! thou strengthener! thou destroyer!
thou refresher of the weary! thou vanquisher
of the strong! thou cheerer of God and man!
thou drink of devils!—thou takest innocent
part in the joy of many a temperate banquet;
and thou scatterest sweet memories and fair
virtues like withered leaves.   Thou bringest
back the gleam of life into the sick man's
eye on his weary bed of pain, and thou art
chief undertaker and hast for thy mourners
broken hearts when dishonoured heads are
laid in drunkards' graves!   We may sit down
to drink with the king and Haman! or we
may fill our glass with the beverage which
has been just taken as from the water-pots
of Cana, at His word who still says at all
temperate banquets, and on all right occasions, "Draw out now and bear to the governor of the feast"!   If you prefer the beverage of the water-pots before the miracle, you
are free! you are right! that too is a gift
of God, the purest and the best.   And there
is much to be said for keeping exclusively to
that—for certainly our modern society is not
quite like a simple rustic marriage company

where there are many guests and little wine.
But if—not despising the water—you feel
that the wine too is yours, then take it, for
yourself and your friends, but under the
shadow of that word as wholesome as it is
solemn, " Let your moderation be known
unto all men—the Lord is at hand."

Many lessons of instruction and warning
might easily be gathered from this chapter.

1st. It shows in a lurid but striking manner *the diabolical character of Revenge.* We
might connect with this the great evil and
danger of pride.   Because revenge is a passion which can exist in any strength only, in
the mind of a man who is proud and selfish.
It is not easy to cast a slight that will be
much felt on a man of *humble* mind.   He
has already the lowly estimate, and although
he may feel that injustice is done him in
particular instances, he will never be thrown
by such things into ungovernable fury, or
drawn into a course of calculated vengeance,
for he will consider in how many things he
is respected beyond what he feels he deserves, and how well it is when it so happens
that there should be some balance.   And in

any case he will content himself with a frank
and fair vindication in the matters where he
is assailed or denied his due. But a proud
and selfish man of necessity becomes malignant and revengeful, and by a kind of brute
instinct will run furiously even upon those
who have done him no injury. There are
names on the roll of history, misnamed
"*great*"—Alexander the Great, Frederick
the Great, Napoleon the Great. No man
can be really great who sports with the lives
and interests of his fellow-creatures—who
can coolly arrange for their destruction by
massacre or in war, simply in order to the
accomplishment of some of his own ambitious
schemes.   Now, you may say that this is
shooting a long way from the mark. *We*
are not Alexanders, Napoleons, Hamans.
Well, I am afraid there is a little touch of
Haman in every one of us. Have you never
heard some one say, have you never said
yourself—"I don't like the family," and you
know nothing about the family, only you
have some grudge, well or ill founded, against
a particular member of it ? Of the rest you
know as little as Haman did of the Jews

whom he wanted to destroy.   Pride is pride,
and revenge is revenge in quality, although
they only show themselves in words with
little stings in them, and by insinuations that
have no *known* ground of verity.   If we do
not make it our business to chastise our
spirits and purify them from the seeds and
shadows of these vices, in the forms in which
they *can* assail us, can we be quite sure that
if we were on the wider stage and had the
ampler opportunity, we should not be as this
devilish Amalekite ?

2d. Without glorifying the character of
this man Mordecai, of whom we really know
very little—he is a dark man—we are bound
I think to believe that his refusal of homage
was—not a freak of spleen and pride on his
part, which would put him in the same cate-
gory with Haman—but in some way a
matter of principle and conscience, and we
have therefore here, legitimately, *a lesson of
personal independence.*   What meanness there
is in this country in bowing down to rank !
in letting some lordly title stand in the place
of an argument ! in seeking high patronage
for good schemes, as men seek the shadow of

broad trees on hot days! in running after royal carriages! in subservience to power, and adulation of wealth! Rise up, Mordecai, in thy Jewish gaberdine, and shame us into manliness, and help us to stand a little more erect! Shades of the Covenanters and spirits of the Puritans, draw not away from us and our relaxed and accommodating ways, and in your great society, and with the memory full upon us of your plain sincerity and uncon- querable courage, we will *not* bow down to what is not true, to what is not honest, to what is not good!

3d. Finally, a lesson of patience and quiet- ness to all the faithful. Obey conscience, honour the right—and then fear no evil.

Is the storm brewing? It may break and carry much away—but it will not hurt *you.* A little reputation is not *you.* A little pro- perty is not *you.* Health even is not *you,* nor is life itself. The wildest storm that *could* blow, would only cast you on the shores of eternal peace and safety.

But more probably the storm may melt all away in a while, and leave you in wonder at your own fears; and, in wonder still deeper before the everlasting wisdom that makes no mistakes, and the infinite tender love that makes all things work for good to the loving heart.   Amen.

LECTURE V.

CHAPTER IV.

DEEPENING TROUBLE.

"THE king and Haman sat down to drink." "It is not for kings, O Lemuel, it is not for kings to drink wine ; nor for princes strong drink : Lest they drink and forget the law, and pervert the judgment of any of the afflicted. Give strong drink unto him that is ready to perish, and wine unto those that be of heavy hearts. Let him drink, and forget his poverty, and remember his misery no more."

But may it not be that the king and Haman *were* among the heavy-hearted that night? and that they drank to forget their miseries ? When a great crime is committed, like that to which they had just put hand and seal—a crime against which humanity herself revolts with

a cry—may it not be that the soul suddenly
shivers as in the winter of moral poverty and
destitution ?   The two most powerful men
in the world that night were cowards before
their own consciences ; and while seated
amid the splendours of the empire, are poorer
than the beggar at their gates.   But here
they sit—while out yonder in the midst of
the city, one clothed in sackcloth and sprink-
led with ashes is rending the air with loud
and bitter cries of grief and consternation.
The same effect is produced everywhere, and
through all the provinces, by the bloody
decree.   " Mourning," " fasting," " weeping,"
" wailing " !   Many lying low, like men dead,
in sackcloth and ashes !

But this man who cries so loudly and
bitterly at the centre of the city has more
occasion and cause than any one else for his
grief and wailing.   For it is by his means—
through his refusal to bow to Haman—that
the whole calamity has come ; and although
he probably does not blame himself for acting as he has done, he cannot but have his
soul stirred with profoundest anguish in looking to the possible consequences of his action.

If you, going from one part of a city to another, were to direct the driver of your hired vehicle to go by one street rather than the one usually taken, and some injury should be done by the wheels of your carriage to some one in the way—in the street of your preference—an old woman lamed, or a child killed—well, it would be very weak to blame yourself for the perfectly innocent choice you had made, as if you had committed sin in making it. But how few would be able to help the melancholy and almost self-reproachful reflection, " O if I had only let the man go his own way !" From a supposition like this, we can judge what a storm of emotion would be surging in Mordecai's breast as he thought of the possible destruction of a whole people—his own people—by his means ! He " came even before the king's gate "—as *near* to the gate as he dared. For none in sackcloth might pass *within* the gate. They that dwell in kings' houses wear *soft* clothing; and use soft speech ; and follow gentle and obsequious ways. Kings' houses are for feasting, and grandeur, and beauty, and display, for the *bright* side of human life.

"Keep the shadows outside the gates. Chase away pain and misery!" And yet misery can fix her fangs in a king's conscience. Pain can write deep lines on kings' faces. Death can "climb up into the windows, and enter into the palaces," while not a gate is unbarred, and not a servant is asked to show the way. And rumour can enter! The queen is kept in the dignity and safety of seclusion; like all the Persian women of high estate. But Esther's maids and chamberlains are in communication with the world, and of course she soon hears of what is taking place among her people, and especially of Mordecai's behaviour. The queen is of course filled with deep concern. But thinking that probably the cause of all this mourning might be something temporary and not worthy of so much notice, and especially grieved that her father (for such he had been to her) should be so prominent in the *demonstration* of the grief—sent raiment to him, with orders to take the sackcloth away. But no! It had not been lightly put on, and cannot be thus put off. This man has a will of his own! He will not bow down to Haman.

He is not to be terrified.   He will not put
off the dolorous robe although *besought* to do
so by one who is both a daughter and a queen!
He is not to be won.   A born ruler of men !

"Then called Esther for Hatach"—that
one of the king's chamberlains who was
specially appointed to be as a lord in waiting
upon her—the queen.   Silently, swiftly, and
very faithfully Hatach did his work.   He
is soon in the street of the city, and being
there he soon finds the man he seeks ; and
delivering his message from Esther, soon
hears from him the whole case in all its black
particulars, and receives from him in return
a narrative and message to the queen which
will chill her blood as she listens to it, which
will melt her whole heart to tears, and then
(if the nobleness is in her, on which Mordecai
seems to count) will harden it into steel for the
deed of daring on which she must venture.

"Go to the queen," saith Mordecai, "thou
faithful Hatach, go instantly, and tell her all;
and take this document, show her the writing,
that her eyes may see on the inhuman page,
as it were, the blood of her people, and that
she may act accordingly !"

She is not, however, left to her own reasonings and conjectures, or even her own impulses, as to what the proper action is to be.
Mordecai decides that for her; decides it
strongly; gives even no alternative; furnishes
therefore no excuse for fears, or opportunity
for natural vacillation; she must go unto the
king to supplicate and make request for the
life of her people—"*And Hatach came and
told Esther the words of Mordecai.*"

Then, probably, came a time of retirement,
of silence, of darkness, of brooding fear, of
heart-searching, and surely (although nothing
of this kind is told us) of prayer to the God
of her fathers.

Again comes forth the queen, pale, tearful,
perplexed, and asks for Hatach, who is again
at hand.   For the time fear seems to have
prevailed in the mind of the queen—fear and
prudence.   The likelihood of success in the
daring enterprise to which she was counselled
appeared to her very, very small.   The likelihood of failure—a failure fatal to her own life,
while in no wise helping to save the life of
her people—appeared very, very large; as
well it might.   He who deposed a queen for

not complying with a personal wish which was rather against the law than otherwise, will he scruple to take the very life of *another* who, bolder still, shall dare to break a law of the empire, an inflexible custom of the court, by appearing in his royal presence unbidden? Undoubtedly the probabilities of the case are on the side of Esther's fears ; and her message now to Mordecai takes shape accordingly.

"Go tell him he is asking me to do what is impossible ; what every one *knows* to be impossible ; what, if attempted, will almost certainly end my days. There is *one* law, and no escape from it. Yes, there is the golden sceptre ; and once I might have had good hope of so moving the heart of the king by the sight of my face, although unbidden, that his hand would have grasped instinctively that sceptre to bid me live ; but there also some shadow has fallen, for I have not been called to see his face for thirty days !"

All which is faithfully and quickly reported to the man in sackcloth on the street ; and one can imagine the disappointment, the anxiety, the resolution which would work in his very features. "Ah, then ! is she failing me—she, the child of so much care, of so much love—and in an hour like this, when the life of all our people is in the balance, when all hell is on the spring ? But it must not be. Her woman's fears must be quelled by that voice of parental authority which once she so gladly obeyed, and which, I think, will be potent with her still. Her queenly courage must be reinforced by showing her the grandeur of the act she is now called on to perform ; and all that is saintly and pious in her must be incited to action by a view of the service which may be rendered to God and His cause !"

Swiftly, therefore, sorrowfully, but sternly, he sends answer back in words which are distinguished for tragic pathos and grandeur, for religious loyalty, for patriotic loyalty to his own people, for unsparing faithfulness to her whom he loved, probably more than any other human creature, and for wide and far-reaching views of providence. In all these respects, and in others, these final words of Mordecai to Esther are wonderful words. " Think not with thyself that thou shalt escape in the king's house more than all the Jews. For if thou altogether holdest thy peace at this time, then enlargement and deliverance to the Jews shall arise from another place ; but thou and thy father's house shall be destroyed. And who knoweth whether thou art come to the kingdom for such a time as this ?" The words took immediate effect ; and that effect exactly the one designed. Indeed one could almost fancy that even during Hatach's absence Esther had thought better of it, had become half ashamed of her fears, had risen in her secret heart more into the heroic mood, and had all *but* resolved to put " her life upon the hazard of the die." For, as far as can be seen, there is no more any hesitation or delay ; and an answer is sent at once to Mordecai, which in all respects is a noble match to his message—in some respects even *more* than a match for it. More devout, more tragic, more noble. He is a man—she is a woman ; he is free—she is little better than a prisoner in her palace ; he can consult with others—she has no heart to answer the sorrow of her own ; his life is not endangered by what he counsels her to do—her life will depend on the mood of a wayward and fitful monarch. Honour, to whom honour ? After all it is Esther who performs the noblest act. She only has the opportunity; but she is equal to it. Serenely, piously, courageously, equal to it. Nothing can be imagined more discreet and beautiful than the whole order and method of her resolution.

First, she wishes Mordecai to secure a fast among all the Jews in the city, to continue for three days and nights, in which she and her maidens would join. This is (we think) an appeal to heaven. True there is no mention of prayer. This is one of the singularities of the book; and Bishop Wordsworth makes it tell to Esther's and Mordecai's disadvantage, and to that of their people. Religiously they had been so deteriorated that they had lost the habit and forgotten the language of prayer, and fell into this custom of fasting in a half superstitious manner. The great body of the commentators, however, take it for granted as a matter about which there can be no doubt that prayer was joined with fasting. Indeed most of them don't seem to notice its absence in the narrative, but simply assert its presence. Good Matthew Henry talks as if the prayer were the thing mentioned, and the fasting the thing to be inferred and explained. Certainly the probability is strong that prayer and fasting were joined. And so the act was solemnly religious—an earnest appeal from helpless human creatures exposed to great peril to the great Ruler, in the full belief that He could arrest the peril, and build a wall of safety about them all. And who shall say how much this time of fasting and prayer contributed to bring about the result? Then the entrance to the king shall take place. And whatever be the issue, there shall be no drawing back! "So will I go in unto the king: and if I perish, I perish!"

And now to close. In addition to the instruction which we cannot fail to obtain, in simply passing in review a narrative like this —so full of human action and passion—there are some points which we may lift up as it were out of the narrative, to be contemplated apart and for their own sakes.

I.

Hatach the chamberlain gives us a good subject for reflection; and not a hackneyed one. Pause we a moment then on this *un*distinguished name. Let the greater actors stand aside—king and queen—Haman and Mordecai—mourning Jews and raging Amalekites—and let a servant (in high office no doubt, but still a servant), rendering true fealty in the spirit of reverence and faithfulness, stand before us in his undistinguished honesty and simplicity. We are not in so many words told that he was honest and true, but we instinctively feel it, and we see that it is involved in the narrative. The queen begins to be in sore trouble. The darkness is deepening. Some unknown but dire calamity is near—" Send me Hatach—I need my truest and my best—'that I may know what it is, and why it is,' and what may be done to prepare for, or avert the evil day."

Imagine, if you can, what this world would be if all the Hatachs were taken out of it, or taken out of its offices. Let Abraham have no Eliezer ; Sarah no Deborah ; Naaman's wife no little maid of Israel ; Saul no armour-bearer ; Esther no Hatach. Let that process go on through a particular section of society, and what helpless creatures kings and

queens would be, and all the men of great
name, and all who live in state, and luxury,
and grandeur ! It would be like a landslip
in society. The upper stratum would come
sliding down, in some cases perhaps toppling
down in many things to a level with the
lowest. Not that the lowest stratum in
society—we mean the great working-class—
has any monopoly of the hard work, and the
consequent merit of upholding what we call
the social scale, or the framework of society.
They are at least as dependent as any other
class. In some senses they are even more
dependent upon others than others are upon
them. There are much harder workers than
the working men ; and if some who are now
high up because they have faculty, industry,
and principle, were, through any social shift,
thrown down, they would be up again to-
morrow, and it would be best for society that
they should be. But none the less on this
account should the privileged classes remember that they lean upon the class next to
them (as of course they in their turn do upon
others), upon the great faithful serving class
of different grades that comes between the

highest and the lowest. There are men in government offices never heard of in public life, who have more merit in particular measures which pass into law than some of those whose names are connected with them. There are managers and confidential clerks who mainly conduct great businesses in the city, and in whom their masters proudly and safely trust. Or, to enter the private scene, many a house is kept quiet and orderly, and sweet and homelike, mainly by the untiring assiduities of one confidential servant—one or more. Let Hatach stand for them all, and give them royal greeting, and one waft of gratefulness as we pass along. Be proud and thankful also any of you who are in the class. To be serviceable and useful in this world, or in any world, is to be great! And "in the regeneration,"—in the rectified time when *men* as well as things shall be put in their proper places, kings and queens for heavenly royalties will be selected from all earthly stations, and lifted sometimes out of very quiet and unseen places, and rulers for celestial cities will be found often in men over whom others have ruled.

II.

Is it too much to say that we may see in the illustrative example of this passage, what may be called the divine meaning and purpose of social elevation ?   It is never brought about in the providence of God, simply for its own sake.

A man is not lifted up into some high place only that he may be seen, talked of, admired, envied.   A woman is not advanced out of simple, girlish life in a quiet home, to shine in a court or move in high circles, or be the possessor of great wealth, only for display, and for what is called the happiness of passing days.   No ; depend upon it, God who has made the ladder for the rise has something worthy and corresponding which the person *may* do when he is at the top.

Some great truth may be witnessed for, some higher duty may be done ; some trial springing out of the advancement, or in some relative way may be brought on by it, may be encountered and endured in such a spirit, and with such effects, that successive generations will enjoy the long benefit.   And yet

how men counterwork God in this! See how
wealth goes into 'showy houses, costly furni-
ture, luxurious feasts, prancing horses, and
all the hum, hurry, and parade of fashionable
life. Among those crowds which fill all the
ways of fashion, there are many gentle, tender
hearts by nature, and many nobler possibilities at least, which are thus neglected, cor-
rupted, and destroyed.

The rules for safety are very simple and
easy. As you get, give. As you rise, fight
the demon of vanity and pride ; grapple
hard and close with the giant sloth. What
the hand finds to do, let it be done. Say
to your soul, "What moral elevations shall
I stand on now ? What service can I
do for those below, for those behind ?
How can I glorify 'the lifter up of my
head ' ?"

III.

The passage reminds us that there is often
in a human life a critical time, when the
whole character is tried and developed in
one way or another ; when the whole life is

thrown this way or that by a single decision
of the will.   Not that every one could find
in his own life anything strictly resembling
this trial, moral and providential trial, of
Esther.   A poor, mechanical use of Scripture
is made, and a very narrow, formal view is
taken of our large and various human life,
when it is insisted that we must each and all
resemble, in this and that, people who lived
and died thousands of years ago.   Still it is
a fact, that in human life there are testing
times, times of crucial severity, and probably
for each *one supreme moment*, when, as we may
say, all is lost or all is won.   That pale,
trembling queen, shrinking back from a
danger which seems too near and certain to
be evaded if she takes one advancing step, is
the image of a doubting, daunted spirit,
arrested or hindered in its higher progress by
the terrors of the world, by strong temptations or allurements, by unworthy loves or
fears.   That pale, trembling, yet adamantine
queen, with her eye on duty now, even when
duty is all but synonymous with death, is the
image of the delivered, resolved soul, when,
emerging from the struggles of the crucial

trial of life, it strives to enter in, and does
enter in at the strait gate, and passes along
the narrow way towards wealth, and large-
ness, and heaven.

IV.

We should not fail to observe what *form*
this supreme trial takes, when it is at the
height ; and what form personal *victory* in it
will take when it is achieved. It is a trial
of life—present life with its pleasures and
advantages : and the victory is achieved by
yielding present life—by giving it away, in
purpose, by " laying it on an altar," as we
say, by " losing it," as saith our Lord Jesus
Christ. "*Now* I am willing to go in," saith
the queen, " and in no craven spirit. And
if I perish, I perish." That is the language
of tried unselfishness—of victorious goodness
—of virtue and religion for every age. And
in the last resort every true soul should be
able, and as we cannot but believe would be
able, to say with Esther, "*If I perish, I perish.*" A lower self is sacrificed, that a higher
self may be vindicated. All is yielded up, if

need be, to be crucified and slain—pleasure, position, life itself, that the true life may live eternally.

V.

And last of all—that none may be discouraged either concerning themselves or their dear friends, remember that there are many lives lived through and ended by death, without opportunity given, at all resembling this in the life of Esther, of declaring and manifesting what *is* the deepest affection, and what the supreme choice would be, if there were a necessity for declaring it. About the truth itself there cannot be, must not be, the shadow of a doubt. "He that loveth his life, shall lose it." He who deliberately takes and keeps his own selfish way—pleasure, advantage, ease, profit, in his eye, while he is blind to highest duty and holiest law of God —he loses all. He soon runs through the present, and there is to him no future to be desired, no treasure bearing interest. "But he that *loseth* his life, for Christ's sake, shall keep it unto life eternal"—giving up all when duty calls. He shall gain all in the

higher sense, and keep what he gains for
ever. About this we say there must be no
mistake : and surely we ought far more than
we do to be trying ourselves by these testing
words. But now, after all, see how few
human beings stand in supreme conspicuous
position before their fellow-creatures, at any
time in their life. How few therefore have
the chance of showing in any dramatic or
decisive way what metal they are made of,
and what or who rules their inward life.
Quietly, kindly, usefully they live, making
many a little sacrifice, which but for Christ
would not be made ; and doing many a
gentle deed, which but for Christ would not
be done ; and sometimes, too, things quite
brave and grand in their way, although
known only to few, and of such a nature
that they never can be spoken about to any
besides. Then quietly and unnoticed by the
great world they die, and are laid in the
grave, loved, lamented, honoured, by those
who knew them best and loved them most.
We claim them also, as pertaining to God's
true sacramental host. All are Christ's who
believe in Christ ! All are Christ's who love

Him! All are Christ's who *can* say or *could* say for His sake and in His strength, " If I perish, I perish!" Perish? You shall never perish if you are thus in Him. His gift is eternal life, and none can pluck you out of His hands. Amen.

LECTURE VI.

CHAPTER V.

THE GOLDEN SCEPTRE.

"TO everything there is a season, and a time to every purpose under the heaven — a time to laugh and a time to weep, a time to mourn and a time to dance ;" and we may add, " a time to fast, and a time to eat and drink and praise the name of the Lord !" Queen Esther's fasting is over ; and although she does not take to feasting, which would, indeed, suit ill with the occasion, she no doubt strengthened herself with what she needed before taking the grand step—the results of which could be known only by taking it.

"Now, it came to pass on *the third day*"— the third day of the passover. The decree for destruction was made "on the thirteenth day of the first month" (see chap. iii. 12)— *i.e.* the day before the passover—and now the first step towards deliverance is to be taken *on the third day* of the passover. An opinion is held by some interpreters (and, considering the strikingly typical character of some parts of Jewish history, it is not easy to say that it is unfounded) that in this great deliverance of the people, and in this recorded destruction of their enemy, and expressly by the means he had devised for *their* destruction, we are to see a distinct foreshadowing of a far grander deliverance : that, viz., which was wrought for the spiritual Israel, the universal church of God, by Him who suffered at the passover and rose again *on the third day*. We may come upon this idea again ; meantime it is well to keep it in mind, if only that we may feel that this narrative is possibly more spiritual, and more *evangelical* even, than a superficial reader would suppose, and that while giving account of the splendours, excesses, and intended cruelties of the Persian court and its grand monarch, advised by a crafty Amalekite, it is truly symbolising

Herod and Pontius Pilate, the Romans and the people of the Jews, under satanic instigation, plotting the destruction of Christ and His kingdom, but finding themselves utterly overthrown by the power of His very cross. The analogy fails in several points ; in others it is close and striking, and whether it be a true and divinely intended analogy or not, the rich natural interest of look will remain for us.

On the third day behold the queen arrayed in " royal apparel ;" or rather, if it were literally rendered, " Esther put on her royalty !" There is no *specific* reference to dress. She put on her queenly *looks* as well as her queenly robes, and entered on her work with all becoming dignity, and no doubt with due attendance—not flurried, or timorous, or indignant, but with seriousness, charm, and grace—in " her royalty." *So* she stands before the king ; " in the inner court," the *very* place over which the special prohibition rests, over which the death-sword hangs, threatening every advancing step. The inner court was the more private residence of the monarch ; yet the king was upon the throne, his sceptre in

his hand, engaged, therefore, probably in some
affairs of state, or concerning his kingly household.   The king sat at the upper end of the
hall, which was always open at the front, so
that he could see all who entered into the
inner court.

He would see Esther almost at the moment of her entrance.   A lord in waiting
might slip in unobserved, but not the queen!
In the Apocryphal book of Esther, it is said
she entered attended only by two maids.
"On one she leaned as carrying herself daintily,
while the other, following, bore up her train.
She was ruddy through the perfection of her
beauty ; her countenance cheerful and smiling, but her heart was in anguish through
fear.   While the king, on his part, clothed
in his robes of majesty, and all glittering with
gold and precious stones, was very dreadful.
As soon as he saw the queen he looked
fiercely upon her, while she, overcome with
terror, grew pale and fainted.   The king, in
an agony, leaped from his throne, took her
in his arms till she came to herself, and then
spake loving words to her, and assured her
she should not die."   That account we may

call, truly, *Apocryphal.* It is little more than a picture of the fancy, designed to produce theatrical effects.

The two maids may be historical. Although there is something also in the idea of a quaint old author, that " it is likely she left her attendants without, lest she should draw them into danger ; and contented herself (when she went in to the king) with those faithful companions, faith, hope, and charity ; who brought her off also with safety." It is more natural and more in consonance with the text of the history to think of her as going into the actual presence, *alone :* "*I and my maids* will fast." " So will *I* go in unto the king." " If *I* perish, I perish ! " At once she stands *alone*, in the place of peril, in the place of hope. And when the king *saw* her, she obtained favour in his sight. The sight of her face in a moment awoke the favourable feeling. As far as appears there was no thunder on the king's brow, no lightning flashes from his eye. The whole process was accomplished in a look. When he *saw* the queen, she obtained favour. If we like to speculate on the possible reasons, there is

I

a wide field of conjecture. The *hour* of the adventure, perhaps, was discreetly chosen. Certainly Esther was not the woman to choose an unfavourable hour if she knew it. Was it after banquet? or after some good news had reached him? or at a time of the day when he was known to be, generally, in an amiable mood?

Or was there something peculiar on her face?—the beauty of the Lord her God upon her; a beauty with solemnity and grandeur in it, like that which sat on Stephen's face when he stood in a danger from which he was not delivered. The same quaint author we have quoted says, " Some faces we know do appear most orientally fair when they are most instamped with sorrow." But a better reason than any other, perhaps, is this, that " the king's heart is in the hand of the Lord, as the rivers of water, and he turneth it whithersoever he will."

It is, however, a constant fact in nature that the sight of a face will do what nothing else can do in the way of awakening love, touching sympathy, securing trust, evoking help, or, it may be, in the way of provoking and stimulating feelings of a very opposite description.   If a purpose be very important, and very good, generally it will be better promoted by a personal appearance than by any kind of representation.   If I am seeking a good thing, my face ought to be better than the face of another for the getting of it ; better, too, than my own letter asking it.   If the poor widow had sent *letters* to the unjust judge, he probably would not have been much discomposed ; but by her continual *comings* she wearied him, and won her quest.

No doubt there are troublesome, pertinacious, unwarrantable comings, as well as industrious, benevolent, and self-sacrificing comings ; and we must distinguish between the one and the other both in the visits we receive and make.   We have no right to set up a tyranny of benevolence, and because *we* are satisfied of the goodness of our aims to force these aims upon the attention of other people. However, our true lesson from the passage and the example of Esther lies on the other side of the subject.   What our hand findeth to do our *own* hand should do, and *not* the hand of another. Personal presence is a power that nothing else can equal—in love, in sickness, in days of peril, for sympathy with suffering, for helpfulness in any kind of difficulty. we all have a king to go in unto ; we all have a possible good to attain which can be reached in no other way but by venturing *ourselves*.

"And the king held out to Esther the golden sceptre that was in his hand, and Esther drew near and touched the top of the sceptre." In reverence, in submission, and for safety, she touched the top of the sceptre, and then all the power of the empire was between her and harm. We cannot assert that this was meant to be a symbolical act ; but certainly it does express in a striking way the method and the result of our coming as sinners to God. The golden sceptre of grace is ever in the King's hand. Never does He cast one wrathful glance upon any who approach unto Him ; He is on the throne of grace, that He may be gracious. When we touch the sceptre we yield submission ; we are reconciled, accepted, and protected by all the forces of the universe, and by all the perfections of God.

"What wilt thou, Queen Esther, and what is thy request?" There is something kindly and auspicious in the naming of the name. "What wilt thou? It shall be even given thee to the half of the kingdom." This is hyperbolical language. It was understood to be so; and any one asking the literal fulfilment of it would have been quite as likely to get *the whole* of the kingdom as the half of it. Herod, indeed, stood to the letter of his shameful promise to the dancing damsel on his birthday; but would he have stood to it still if she had asked for his own head in a charger, instead of John the Baptist's? There must always be a limit understood, if not expressed. As also in the case of the far grander promises of God to his children, when he says, "All things are yours." That is true within its own proper limits; "all things are ours" as far as we need them, and can receive them. Esther knew quite well that the king's words were not to be literally taken; and although she was not going to ask for half the kingdom, or, indeed, for *any* of the kingdom strictly speaking, she yet felt that her request—the request she was about to prefer

—was sufficiently serious to demand her utmost prudence in the way of presenting it.
Nothing, in fact, in its way can be more
admirable than the queen's self-possession and
thoughtful prudence in this part of the business. Many a woman, of more impulsive
temperament, would have seized on the king's
promise as soon as uttered, and would have
impeached the enemy of her race publicly and
passionately before the very throne. But no;
there were reasons sufficient against that
method. For one thing, Haman does not
seem to have been present—not in close
attendance at this time—and she wishes to
charge him to his face. Or she knew that
the king would be more likely to listen at the
banquet which (again with womanly fore-
thought) she had already prepared, and to
which she now, with all respect and humility,
ventures to invite the king. " The king and
Haman !" " Let the king and Haman come !"
"Ah ! then she thinks of him whose society I
most enjoy, whom I most delight to honour.
Yes; let Haman come with me to the banquet,
and cause him to make haste. We will go
now !"

And to the banquet they came. The king pleased and propitious, Haman exultant.

Esther's banquet, although no doubt costly and splendid, and suitable to the occasion, would not in any respect, except perhaps beauty and tastefulness, vie with the great royal banquet which went on in the Persian palace *every* day.   Not less than a thousand victims bled daily to furnish forth the tables of the palace itself and of all who were connected with it — servants, guards, soldiers, satellites.   Esther's banquet was probably little more than fruit and wine.   Possibly the king had just dined, and was as ready as any modern prince or merchant would be for the banquet of wine.

See, he is now in the queen's drawing-room, shall we say ?—reclining on a couch with golden feet, taking sips now and again of the golden water which was specially prepared, and of which he and his *son* alone might drink, and then, as the banquet went on, drinking freely of the wine.   Haman is on the ground, no doubt on a rich mat or carpet.   The queen, too, has her couch and

her royal attendance ; but to-day, as we may
well suppose, is concerned chiefly that the
king shall be thoroughly pleased. He *is*
well pleased. For soon he makes request,
in the same language he had used when the
golden sceptre was in his hand, to know the
queen's petition, and gives the same promise
that it " shall be granted, even to the half of
the kingdom."

But, strange to say, Esther is not yet
ready to speak it out. Was there, after all,
a something in the king's aspect which made
her pause ?—or was it that she had not yet
fully decided on the *best* method of unfolding
the case ?—or was it that she would engage
the king's affection, if possible, more strongly
on her side by a *second* banquet, and by all
the charms she herself could throw around it ?
Or was it that she would heighten the
importance of the communication, to the
king's apprehension, by delaying it ? Or
was it that her heart misgave her at the
last moment, and she shrank, in womanly
fear, from the revelation which yet was beat-
ing and burning in her breast ? Or rather,
was it not, like so many other things in this

history, a wise and striking providence of God making use of some of these human feelings and secondary things to *obtain needed delay*, in order that other things might come in, the things narrated in the next chapter?

This last is the true answer. In this history, pre-eminently one thing is interwoven with another, is dependent on another. Looking superficially on the matter, you would say, There can be no need of delay ; *already* there has been delay ; and the very hour has now come, and this is the place to divulge the secret. The very persons are here before whom it *will* be told to-morrow—-the king, the queen, Haman! Then why delay? Nine people out of ten would have said, if consulted beforehand—" Ah, she is losing her case, through fear or through finesse, or by some evil counsel. She is losing the ripe and favourable hour, which will never return. To-morrow! O Queen, why not to-night?" And so, oftentimes, we would hasten providence in our own affairs, fretting against His wise delays, and laying our poor shoulders to the great wheels of God, as though He were not moving them fast enough, when, in fact,

they are going as evenly as the sun, as sublimely as time itself. " The king is here ;
why not speak ? "   Yes, he is here, and he is
not here.   He is *not* here as he will be to-
morrow night.   To-night he will be sleepless.
To-night he will be reminded, through his
sleeplessness, of an act of loyal faithfulness
on the part of Mordecai, which has been
hitherto unrewarded.   To-night the order
will be given for the preparation of a gallows.
In a word, when the same three meet at to-
morrow's banquet, they will be the same, and
yet *not* the same.   They will be really in
different relations to each other, and to many
beyond.   So the banquet is ended, as if by
the utterance of the word, " wait."   " He that
believeth shall not make haste."

   Haman makes haste home with a glad
heart.   What a step in advance he has made
now !   King and queen vying with each
other to do him honour !   " Let the king and
Haman come to-morrow," said the queen
when he took his leave.   " Joyful and with
a glad heart " he passes through the gates
towards his house.   And as he goes along
there is, as heretofore, universal reverence

most obsequiously made. All rise as he comes, and bow low as he passes by. All except one. And in a moment he knows that one. His secret soul is on the watch, instinctively, for the hated form of Mordecai. His enmity is so deep and constant, that it would be almost a disappointment to him if that form were not there. But there it is—to his jaundiced vision " squat like a toad "—or crouching like a tiger in his lair! although it is likely that Mordecai was sitting calmly enough —possibly with some thoughts in heaven seeking help there for all this earthly trouble. But there he sits, certainly, and will not rise. If a controversy like this is worth beginning, it is equally worth continuing to its proper end. Haman's brow darkens as he passes, his heart beats faster. Rage possesses him, and runs like fire through his veins. His very fingers itch and feel like fangs which he would gladly fix in strong death-grip in the heart-strings of his enemy! He was full of indignation.—But " he refrained himself." There *was* a danger then that he might break out against him there and then ! That he might play the king for the nonce, or

feign the king's authority and cry, " Have
that vile caitiff away to instant execution."
But this would have been too high a game
to play, and a salutary fear of the highest
authority kept him in check—all the more
that he felt persuaded that he could, in a day
or two, accomplish, in one way or other, his
fell purpose under the sanction of the law.

So now he is *home !* Yes, that word
" Home " is used about Haman's house—
that word which is in some ways more
musical than any other—which is all full of
balm, and blessing, and kindness, and gentleness, and grace !   How much of all this there
was in Haman's house, it would be harder
than some would imagine to tell.   That
wretch Nero, who came perhaps as near absolute fiendishness as a human being could,
had *some* who seemed almost to love him.
When he fled from Rome, chased by universal execration, and took refuge in the house
of a freedman, an old and faithful nurse followed and ministered to him !

Haman had a wife Zeresh, said by the
Targum to be the daughter of Tatnai, the
Persian governor on the western side of the

Euphrates. He had ten sons—how many daughters we know not, daughters were little thought of in those times. He had friends also, most of them no doubt fair-weather creatures, possessing like riches good strong wings to flee away with when occasion shall come. But, as this world goes, very good friends to-day. And they hasten at the great man's call to his house; expecting no doubt to hear some very special tidings of the queen's banquet, and what came of it, and certainly *not* expecting to hear any *complaint* from Haman's lips. Nor do they for a while. He began a kind of set speech to them, the subject of which was himself! His wealth, his children, his honours, are all dilated upon, carefully put into a narrative for a purpose. Nor does the proud and vain man forget to add the crowning circumstance, the very last that had occurred, that he *alone* had been allowed to go with the king to the queen's banquet; and that he brought an invitation home with him from the queen herself that he should to-morrow repeat the visit. And now comes the purpose of this long and vain-glorious narrative. It is to give weight to a most dolorous complaint, to tell them in fact that "all this avails him nothing, so long as he sees Mordecai the Jew sitting at the king's gate." In all history perhaps we have no more striking instance of the utter insufficiency of the very highest forms and fullest measures of worldly good to secure individual happiness — the happiness of a worldly man! One thing lacking, or one thing present and irrevocable, makes a hundred other things of no avail! One fly in the ointment makes it to send forth a stinking savour, at least to the dainty nostril. Ahab wears a crown and rules a kingdom, and yet, failing to get a vineyard which he coveted, from poor Naboth the owner, he takes to his bed and will eat no bread! Ten thousand men will rise up to Haman when he appears in the city—but the fact that *one* will not, is enough to poison his peace and make him completely miserable.

And the whole boastful narrative is really an appeal to his friends and to his wife to help him out of the misery by giving him wise counsel and advice. They were not

long in consultation. They had no difficulty.
To them the case was clear. It would be a
degradation to Haman to *speak* to such a
man, or to make any farther endeavours to
bring him to a better state of mind. He
has forfeited his life. Listen to the judgment
of these friends in council : " Let a gallows
be made—a wooden tree—a cross in fact—
50 cubits high !—about 75 feet, higher than
any ordinary house ; intended to be so that
it might be seen from afar, over the whole
city ; and that it might proclaim as long as
it stood Haman's victory and Mordecai's
shame." " Let a gallows be made, and *to-
morrow* speak thou unto the king, that
Mordecai may be hanged thereon." Swift
and terrible is the doom thus designed. No
doubt they meant that he should be seized
at once—in the night—asleep, and held
ready for execution in the morning. " Then
go thou in merrily with the king unto the
banquet !" " There will be no Mordecai sitting at the gate going in or coming out !
No plots hatched among your enemies. No
more opposition to your sway."

And this judgment is spoken by the wife

to the husband !   In calling the council
Haman. called his friends, *and* his wife.   It
may be a matter of no real import this
arrangement ; but if he did entertain any
doubt of his wife's ability to grapple with the
merits of a stern case like this, and with un-
shrinking nerve to proclaim the issue, he is
mistaken.   She is equal to the occasion.
Her policy is the firmest ; she is the first in
reply.   One hopes that the first idea and
suggestion of the gallows did not come from
her.   But there is no telling.   A woman of
high capacity, of strong nerve, and milk of
human kindness turned to gall, is terrible!
Jael with the nail and the hammer standing
over the sleeping trustful guest, is a dreadful
picture.   Jezebel half-scornfully saying to
her husband, " Dost thou now govern the
kingdom of Israel ? "   " *I* will give thee the
vineyard of Naboth ! "   And here, Zeresh,
of whom this is all we know, " You shall go
merrily to the banquet to-morrow ! "   Lady
Macbeth is not a historic character.   She is
a creation of high poetic genius.   But she is
no exaggeration of what a *few* women have
been and done in human history.   We can-

not help making the supposition that Shakespeare, in portraying that grand terrific creature, had in view, among others, these scriptural portraits of awful women.

Jael cried to Barak, "Come, and I will show thee the man whom thou seekest," and she took him into the tent and showed him Sisera lying dead, with the nail in his temples! Jezebel said, "*I* will get your vineyard. It is but that an innocent man shall be stoned to death!" Zeresh—"Go *merrily* to the banquet!" Lady Macbeth to her relenting husband—"I have given suck, and know how tender 'tis to love the babe that milks me: I would, while it was smiling in my face, have plucked my nipple from his boneless gums, and dashed the brains out— had I so sworn, as you have done to this."

The truth is women are the best and the worst. Because they can be the best, they can be the worst. Because they can rise to the highest in moral grandeur, in self-sacrificing love, in the things which bring human nature nearest to the angelic mood, therefore they can sink to the lowest, and when "past feeling" can be most like the angels fallen.

K

Nor let all this kind of reflection seem to be too far away from us. Remember such scriptural expressions as these :—" *Of one blood !*" " *Of like passions,*" and that they tell both ways. The saintliest of the saints are to be imitated and followed with all our desires and endeavours, as those whom we may overtake, and of whom we may be the spiritual associates in a while. And the darkest and most abandoned of men and women are to be pitied indeed, but also feared, and regarded with a sensitive and shrinking aversion as those into whose dark company we *might,* by circumstances, be drawn. Thank God if you have a wife or a husband who would give you merciful, and not malignant, counsel, if in any conflict you were ever brought into straits. Thank God if your friends are of milder temper, as no doubt they are, than Haman's. Thank God that your best friends would renounce your society rather than stand by you in anything revengeful or mean.

We all have reason to thank God for our lot, and for the falling of the lines in places so pleasant. How little need have we to

envy the rich, the great, the titled, the powerful! How *much* occasion to be pleased with
quietness, even with commonness, and all the
benign obscurities of ordinary life! Better
so shall we find the sure pathway to heaven.
We have no need to envy our own great men
—not even when they are good. See how
they are suspected, maligned, and tossed from
places they have adorned by unsuspected
ecclesiastical and political combinations, and
how every writer in the daily press thinks it
necessary to "weigh them in his balances
and find them wanting."

If any of us were called to stand in
high place, and render great public service,
and if we had the requisite capacity, we
should no doubt find motive enough to do
our work, even in the face of strong criticism
and constant misjudgments. But we may
well enough be thankful that we have not
the ability, or that having the ability, few of
us are called in God's providence to anything
beyond the more or less even tenor of an
ordinary life.

If we feel rightly, no life will be dearer to
us than common life, and it may well be that

no companionship or society could be more really profitable to us than those we find among what are termed common people. Great people are spoiled for the life that most men must lead. Life becomes policy, watchfulness, ingenuity, reserve. In common life it is *easier* to be simple, sincere, sympathetic, helpful, loving, and easier to find the narrow consecrated way that leads through earth to heaven. Of all the myriads this day in heaven, an immense preponderance in numbers must have been prepared for it in what are called common scenes, and must have gone to it by unseen and undistinguished paths. The chosen disciples and friends of the Son of God were fishermen and vinedressers. God's chosen sons and daughters, those with whom He will hold eternal fellowship in higher scenes, are found—where? Many of them in lowliest places. In cottages, in huts, in desert tents. In small houses of narrow streets. In crowded ships. Remember it is the little child only that enters into His kingdom. Remember it is the lowly who have the promise of grace. Remember that the meek are the largest proprietors, being inheritors of all the earth ; and that it is the poor in spirit who have title and preparation for the kingdom of heaven.

LECTURE VII.

Chapter VI.

THE SLEEPLESS NIGHT.

"ON that night, could not the king sleep." How many different causes or occasions there may be of the sleepless night! Some cannot sleep in the remembrance of recent sin. Some are kept waking by great sorrow. Some by brain excitement. Some in very weariness of over-work. Some, "through the multitude of business," don't get even the length of the "dreams" which haunt the pillows of others. In a comparative sense we may say, "Happy are those who dream," for that shows that they are asleep.

Without staying to construct even the briefest homily on sleep, we may well, in passing on, pause for one moment in grateful recognition of this immense benefit which comes to the human race with the sinking of every sun.   Without it human life would soon come to an end.   It would burn rapidly away.   With unfailing regularity this great boon comes—" Tired nature's sweet restorer, balmy sleep."   But it comes with most regularity and in greatest abundance to those who live the simplest and most regular lives. " The sleep of the labouring man is sweet whether he eat little or much ; but the abundance of the rich will not suffer him to sleep." We do not know, however, that the sleeplessness of Ahasuerus was caused by over-indulgence.   It may have been so : or it may not. More probably it came through some public cares.   Says an old author concerning sleep, They are likeliest for it, who, together with their clothes, can put off their cares, and say, as Lord Burleigh did when he threw off his gown, " Lie there, Lord Treasurer."   Did some flitting shadows bear the king company home from Esther's banquet ?   Was he troubled by her strange request for delay ? Half afraid of the unknown future—of some

possible perils which might be lurking even in
his court, and through the unexpected delay
might break out this very night? We know
not. But here at least is a wonderful thing—
a man who, in kingly rule, commands an hundred and twenty and seven provinces cannot
command an hour's sleep! Ah, great monarch, see how the happy slave released from
the daily task and yoke, and the little infant
who cannot yet shape conscious thought, can
go so easily sailing into the placid realm
which to-night is fast shut against thee!

If the king cannot sleep, how can he best
spend the time? They say it was usual with
the ancient monarchs of the East to call for
instruments of music to beguile the sleepless
hour, and by some soothing strains to lull
them into slumber at last. Nothing of this
kind was proposed; nor anything in the
shape of amusement. Somehow it comes
that the king is in no trivial mood to-night.
Neither singers, nor players, nor actors, nor
dancers, nor readers of the lighter kind of
literature, whatever that may have been, will
be welcome to-night. "Something must be
read. Yes, I shall have an hour of reading;

but it must be something that is true, serious, and with a meaning in it—bring the book of the records of the Chronicles." This record seems to have been a *public* book, written apparently by official authority, and by the historians of the court—a book of reference, from which the reigning monarch might read or not read as he chose. Some think Ahasuerus had never read in it before. It seems more likely, however, that he had, although perhaps but seldom. Some, too, think that the reading was simply to beguile the time, and, if possible, induce slumber. And if reading then had anything like the monotonous, soporific sound, which reading often has now, the specific would not be a bad one. Rather, however, we interpret the king's mood and purpose to be altogether more serious. Not, indeed, that he has any idea of what is going to come of it: what comes of it is purely in the providence of God. But his thoughts are about his kingdom when he calls for the records. And they are read, probably by one of the princes. Of course it could be only a small part of those records that could be read in an hour or two of that sleepless night. The wonder is that the reader fell upon the particular passage or chapter which narrated the king's danger from conspiracy, and his happy escape from it through the loyalty and faithfulness of Mordecai. "The book opened at this particular place," say some of the Jewish doctors, and continued so—"The eye of the courtly reader falling upon the narrative, and his judgment telling him that the incident was most unsuitable to be read to the king in his present nervous and apprehensive condition, he turned to other parts, but still the book or roll continued to open itself at the one place!" Of course we reject that fable; but we must accept the wonderful fact that, *some way or other*, the book did so open at that place. Out of hundreds of chapters to choose from, *this* was the one that came. Probably other things *preceded* this in the reading. It was the last that came; and it came with some power to the monarch's heart. Some way or other he had not thought much about it before, but he thinks the more of it now. Now, in the night, susceptible, excited, secretly alarmed as he is without knowing of any specific cause for the fear, a circumstance like this impresses itself indelibly upon his mind. "Was I indeed so near to death, by the treacherous hands of vile assassins, who had promised to be my special protectors? and was I saved by a stranger's faithfulness—by one who had received no royal favours, and who did what he did in simple honesty and truth? What has been done to that man? What honour and dignity has he received for this? Ah now I bethink me how I *meant* to reward him, but how in the pressure of things the purpose was postponed! I thought he would be sure to come forward *expecting* reward, and I should thus be reminded of his claim; but surely he has not been altogether forgotten! My senators and chief men must have given him something—emolument or office in the way of recompense. *What* honour and dignity hath been done to Mordecai for this?" And the king's servants answer, "There is nothing done for him!"

"Nothing has been done to him! Nothing?" It pleases the monarch ill. It reflects on his accustomed liberality—on the liberality of

the throne, for *all* the Persian monarchs were
open handed. This very monarch gave
Megabyzus for his good service at Babylon
a golden mill weighing six talents. Themistocles, the famous Greek, had three cities and
above two hundred talents of him —" and
nothing done in recognition of a brave and
beneficial action like this?"—Well might I
be sleepless while such a service remains unrewarded—" Who is in the court?" He hears
a footfall and the rustle of garments, as if
some one had just come in. " Some one in
the court?" Why then, it must be morning
—early morning, the dawning of the day.
The night has worn away, the first part of it
in sleepless tossings and anxious thoughts, the
next in listening to that arresting and strangely
forgotten tale. And now the east is rosy,
and morning is climbing the mountain-tops,
and shedding down some awakening glow
into the sleeping valleys and athwart the
vast plains. And some one has come thus
early to be, if possible, the *first* who shall
secure the monarch's ear, when he shall be
pleased to give audience. " Who is in the
court?" " Haman is in the court." What,

so early? Yes. For truth to say Haman too has had a sleepless night, and with more occasion. A fire of hatred and revenge burning fiercely in the breast is not likely to induce sleep. And just when he is falling over there comes again and again through the night air the sound of hatchet and hammer, and he knows too well the meaning of the sound. That gallows is rising in the darkness—higher and higher yet—and now he is here in the dawn to make sure that the hated man shall hang on it. "Haman is in the court." "And the king said, Let him come in." And now again they are together.

Think, I pray you, for a moment, how much depends on who shall speak the first word! Suppose the king had said to his prime minister, as he very well might, "My lord, you have come early. You have something to ask. Freely speak your request." And then suppose Haman, pouring into the monarch's ear, skilfully, as he knew so well how to do, his indictment against Mordecai, pressing the charge most heavily, perhaps not on personal grounds, but because he would make him out to be a deep designing enemy of crown and kingdom——in such a case I say, who knows whether Mordecai might not have hung fifty cubits high in the light of that morning sun ?   No doubt Haman had men, armed and ready, waiting but for the sign to have it all done.   But it is not so to be. Haman must wait.   The king's trouble comes first to-day.   There must be no more delay. No other things must *now* press in until justice is done to a neglected man.   " Tell me, my Lord Haman, what shall be done to the man whom the king delighteth to honour ?"   Alas, poor Haman ! how misleading the question, and how little thy king knows what a tumult of ambition it will stir in thy breast ; and what visions of glory it will bring up before thine eyes !   At this point we almost pity Haman.   If our sympathies do not go to his side, they are at least for the time suspended. There is a kind of tantalising cruelty in the king's speech, although it is not in the least so intended by him, and we watch Haman as we should watch a bird drawing nearer to the snare, or some fierce beast falling unsuspectingly into the hunter's toils.

" To whom," saith he in his heart, " *more*

than to myself, would the king delight to do
honour?" It must be so; of late I have
not had a serious rival. All has been coming
into my hands. And now—What? when
so much is in my power? Money? I have
enough, or can get it easily. A distant city
to rule! I wish to live here in the chief city
of all. A title! I have already a great
name and a great place, and nothing less
than *this* is suited to the case, that I should
now put on, at least, some outward show of
royalty itself, and be *seen* of the people in
such monarchic splendour through the whole
city. The people, after seeing me in this
royal array, may begin to think — Who
knows, who knows, what they may think? It
is not for me to lose the great chance which
is thus brought to my hand." Then he gave
his counsel—that there should be accorded
to this unknown man, about whose identity,
however, he had a joyful presentiment, a
triumphal, and in some sort *royal* progress
through the city, mounted on the king's
horse—the horse which was reserved exclusively for the king's use — clad in royal
apparel, which was very gorgeous, consisting,

in part, of a magnificent turban, of a diadem of white and purple colour, of a rich purple stole or robe of state, reaching down to the heels, covered with gold and precious stones, and symbolical pictures of various living creatures ; a rich cassock, with golden girdle, and, indeed, all of costly barbaric splendour that could be put upon a human person.

Wearing the crown, or rather the meaning seems to be, having the crown borne in the procession so conspicuously that it might be seen that the king gave the most complete sanction to it.   He hardly could have proposed to put *the crown* on any head but the king's ; and it is in conformity with this that the king, in his reply, mentions the apparel and the horse, but says nothing of the crown.

There can be no doubt that Haman means the whole to be a stupendous stroke in his personal policy for advancement, and that he means, at least, to *suggest* to the common imagination certain possible eventualities which he would have shrunk from putting into language—" Admiring peoples, behold ! If ever a monarch should be needed, you know where to find him !"

The counsel is given, and the great man, simulating indifference, perhaps even affecting humility, waits for the reply. · He has not long to wait, probably not many moments. "Yes; thou hast said well. Make haste, and let it all be done, even as thou hast said, *to Mordecai the Jew that sitteth at the king's gate!*" Alas, poor Haman! This answer, so joyously and hopefully waited for, is a sword in thy vitals, is a rope around thy neck; and none the less fell and fatal that thy king, in speaking, means it not so, knows nothing of thy secret feuds and passions, of thy secret hopes and expectations. And this surely must be the special bitterness of the case to thee, that thou hast thyself woven the rope for thine own neck, fashioned the sword which will cut thee to the quick. It is thine own overblown pride, thine own vast ambition, thine own devilish enmity, which thus came back upon thee with tremendous recoil.

The contrasts are wonderful between what was expected and what thus comes. They are drawn out by an old author thus—"Now he must perforce honour him whom he had hoped to have hanged; clothe him whom he

hoped to have stript ; help him up to his
horse upon whose grave he hoped to have
danced ; prepare a triumph for him for whom
he had prepared a tree ; make proclamation
before him as a crier, lead his horse as a
lacquey, do all offices for him as a slave or
underling—oh, what a cut, what a cordolium
was this to a man of his mettle and making !"
And there was no time to get out of it.   It
must be done *now*—in this early morning
time, before the heats of day come on.   Make
haste.   If he could but have had a short hour
to think it all through, and see where he
stood ! and to consult that gentle wife of his
and those friends who, by the vigour of their
counsels, have helped him into this trouble, if
perchance they might help him out of it—
but no.   The whole matter must be transacted
before he can see their faces.   And done it
was.   Josephus says that Mordecai thought
Haman mocking him when he came to him
with the robes, and the horse, and the triumphal pomp, and said unto him, sorrowfully,
but with unbroken courage, "Thou most
wicked man, dost thou thus insult over the
miserable ?"   But being assured that it was

in truth the king's pleasure, he suffered him
to do it.   How Haman did it—really got
through with it—is one of the wonders of the
case.   Yet what will not a man do for safety
and life ?   Disobedience was not possible to
a kingly command so express and urgent.
It was done ; and Mordecai came again
to the king's gate ; and Haman hasted to
his house, mourning and having his head
covered.

That procession through the Persian capital, conducted and managed by the great
Amalekite prince, in honour of the despised
Jew, is, in some ways, perhaps the most
remarkable that ever took place in history.
There is nothing else like it.   Two or three
hours would finish it.   But it has been teaching the world some striking and much-needed
lessons ever since ; and it will continue to
teach them as long as the world lasts—
as long at least as there are good and
bad men in the world, and ups and downs
in life, and a providence of God working
in all.

I.

It teaches us how well a good man can afford to wait for the due acknowledgment of his uprightness, and for any reward he may need for the good he has done. The conjecture is that six long years had gone by since Mordecai revealed the plot of the chamberlains and saved the king's life, and not even a word of acknowledgment had come to him during all that time. At first he would naturally look for something of the kind, for it was usual, it was kingly, on such occasions to confer honours and give rewards ; but as time went on expectation would, of course, diminish, and finally, in all probability, die away, so that when acknowledgment and reward come none is more surprised than he who had ceased to expect them. But what we most admire is his behaviour meantime. If he had been a self-seeking man, he could easily have found means to refresh the king's memory as to his services ; but he kept silence. If he had been a malignant man, he might have sought what he would, in that case, have called a just revenge for the ungrateful neglect with which

he had been treated, by hatching or falling in
with some other plot.   But no ; he keeps his
place, and does his office at the gate quietly
and faithfully, and without fail, expecting
nothing, complaining of nothing, faithful to
duty, and fearing God.   And then, how well
all turns out in the end !   How much better
than if the reward had been given at the time!
Suppose he had got some gift or office at the
time, the answer to the king's question could
not have been, " Nothing has been done for
him ;" and Haman's plot would not have been
arrested, but would have rolled on, on wheels
of fire, towards the destruction of a whole
people.   " He that believeth shall not make
haste ;" God's time is always the best.   Six
years are to the Lord as so many moments.
And God's method of reward and acknowledgment is the best too.   Seldom, indeed,
does it take in the case of any of his servants
a form so dramatic as this.   We misapprehend
and degrade the dramatic element in this
history if we crave the repetition of it.   It is
brought out here in such tragic splendour in
order that the great *moral truth* may be
stamped deeply in human memory, and may

stand out vividly to the human imagination.
You have done some good things in your time
which have never been acknowledged, or never
adequately rewarded, even as such things go
among men.   Even a few frank kindly words
from the proper quarter would have been
something. As it is you are sometimes a little
chilled and discouraged by what you feel to
be the complete and unwonted neglect. Well,
now, don't expect Haman at your door some
fine morning with the king's horse, and the
royal apparel to make you all purple and gold,
and the blaring trumpets to tell all the city
what you have done; he is not likely to come;
you must do as you can without him. Righteousness is its own reward, and we are never
righteous as God would have us be until we
feel this deeply and act accordingly.   If we
stipulate for so much silver and gold, for so
much social respect, for a star on the breast
or a ribbon on the arm, or a horse at the door,
wherein does our righteousness differ from
that of the Scribes and Pharisees, which can
take no man into a kingdom of heaven ?
True, these things *may* come, may be expected to come, under the general laws of

God; but in very various degree. We must leave them to come in God's own time and way. He who, in God's strength, looks every day on the face of duty, and walks with her along whatever paths her sacred feet may tread, has in his own spirit, in his own character, what soon or late will blossom out into all beauty and grandeur ; what will in the end become " glory, honour, and immortality."

II.

The next lesson is just the opposite of this, viz., " How certainly a bad man must be overtaken and punished !" We say " how certainly " because there is *in* his badness the root and element of the retribution, and often, without knowing it, he carefully develops and ripens by his own action the retribution that falls on his head. It is *he* who treasures up wrath against the day of wrath. It is not that there is a watching God with lightnings sleeping all about his throne, and thunderbolts ever ready to his hand. It is rather that evil brings its *own* penalty, that passion bears its own punishment, and that

that punishment often comes along the very line or channel which some particular passion had elaborately prepared for its own gratification. Yet here again, as in the opposite case, let no one expect that in any particular instance there shall be in providence *conspicuous* judgment, and that where such judgment does not come, there is either no wickedness to be punished, or, an escape of that wickedness from the penalties that *ought* to alight upon it. No thought could be more shallow or untrue. Impunity? There is none in working evil, or in being evil. Oh, it is not Haman's open disgrace in being lacquey to the man he despised—it is not even the gallows fifty cubits high, on which we know he will hang, that constitutes his sorest punishment. It is the deadened sensibility, the seared and withered heart, the victorious selfishness, the passions "set on fire of hell," and burning in the breast until no tender precious thing can live—it is a state of things like this which makes the deepest darkest doom, a doom from which only God's great grace can deliver a man when he begins to sink into it. For—

III.

there is an increscent power in evil (as indeed
there is also in good), in view of which we cannot be too watchful and anxious, lest by any
means we should fall under the power of it.
The power of it, remember, is very silent and
gentle, generally, in its operations.   The use
of strong metaphors to signify the growth of
evil is apt to mislead and deceive us.   And
the contemplation of very strong human instances like this of Haman is apt enough to
have the same effect.   The growth of evil—
Do not figure it by the waters of Niagara,
hurrying down the rapids, and plunging over
the brink in ocean fulness.   Take rather a
plant or slender tree in your garden, which
has just begun to grow.   There it stands in
the morning sunlight.   There it stands in the
evening dew.   It never travels, never plunges,
never roars.   *It is growing*—and that is
enough.   So do not look at Haman reeling
on the giddy eminence he is trying to scale,
and falling thence, as Satan did from heaven.
But look at a man growing up in perfect
quietness, who has no care to grow up in real

goodness, no fear of growing up in evil—and there you have the picture, which would be to us, if we could see things as they are, as alarming as any other. Anything may come out of that—Haman, Ahitophel, Judas Iscariot.

Here is the strength, and here is the fitness of the gospel, and here its inestimable preciousness—that it goes to the root of all evil in man. It is a regeneration, a renewing, a quickening, a redemption; when it comes in power it is death to the principle of evil within—considered as the reigning power of the life. "We are crucified with Christ;" and with Christ we attain to "the resurrection of the dead." O happy change that puts us for ever on the winning side; that gives us the pledge and assurance of eternal victory by the attainment of eternal goodness. Is it wonderful that we should exhort sinful men to flee to Him, and to trust Him to the uttermost? In Him we are in the undecaying strength—in the perfect purity—in the infinite love—and therefore in the eternal blessedness.

LECTURE VIII.

From CHAPTER VI. Verse xii. to end of CHAPTER VII.

ESTHER'S SECOND BANQUET.

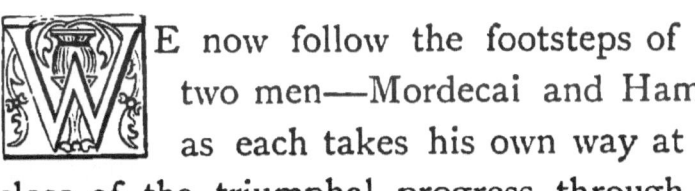

E now follow the footsteps of the two men—Mordecai and Haman, as each takes his own way at the close of the triumphal progress through the city. All that is told us of Mordecai, is that "*he came again to the king's gate.*" But how much is in that! How clearly the *character* of the man comes out in that single touch of description—that one item of information given us, that he came again to the king's gate. A proud ambitious man would have said to himself, " No more of the king's gate for me ! I shall direct my steps now to the king's palace, and hold myself ready for honour, office, emolument, which surely must now be at hand." Mordecai seems to have said with himself, "*If* these things are designed for me in God's good providence, they will find me. But they must seek me, for I shall not seek them. Those who confer them know my address. 'Mordecai, at the king's gate,' will still find me. Let the crowd wonder and disperse. I have had enough of their incense. Let Haman go whither he will, he is in the hands of the Lord. Let my friends at home wait; they will hear all in time. It is as yet no day of triumph for them or me. That dark cloud of peril yet hovers over us both. We must wait. I can wait best at the old place and in the accustomed way—'*at the king's gate.*'"

As for Haman—as soon as the ceremony is over he hastens to his house, mourning, and with covered head. The covered head is the appropriate symbol and expression of the deepest grief and trouble.

What a company was that which David led out of Jerusalem when he fled from his son Absalom in the conspiracy! "David went up," we read, "by the ascent of Mount Olivet, and *wept* as he went up, and had his

head covered, and he went barefoot : and all
the people that were with him, covered every
man his head, and they went up, weeping as
they went up!" The sorrow of that company, however, was but, as it were, for a
night, and joy came to them in the morning.
Haman's sorrow is of a darker kind, and alas,
will grow darker still, and deepen for him into
the night of death. He is soon home, and
soon pours out the tale of his grief to his
listening wife and to his many friends. " He
told them *all that had befallen him !*" Well,
it really was not in itself very much. "All
that had befallen him " that morning would
to many a one have been only an honour,
and to himself, if he had been just and humble,
it would have been no disgrace. But a man's
character gives character to all that befalls
him. Things are this, or that, as the man is.
As the man is, especially, so will be his house.
It may be rest to him and refreshing, and joy
—in one word it may be " *home* "—or, it may
be, what, alas ! Haman's is, flattery, and falsehood, and beguilement, in the days of evil pro-
sperity—and then frost, and winter, and darkness, and judgment, when adversity draws on.

Now, if ever, surely is the time for Zeresh to be the woman and the wife! and for the friends whom Haman has honoured and feasted to show themselves friendly! And we cannot help some emotion of repugnance and even contempt for them, when we see how ready they are to veer round with the shifting wind; and how easily, and without one manly effort to arrest the course of things, they can give up the falling man to destruction. Their behaviour, however, is not *wholly* accounted for by meanness. It is in part the fruit of superstition. The omens had changed. Right and wrong, cruelty and kindness—those were not the things which guided and warned them. They had been guided by the auspices, by the king's smile, by the growing influence, and honour, and wealth of their chief, and when these are changed, all is changed. The fates are changing—the gods are changing. Very ungodly people are sometimes very superstitious. And yet perhaps their belief *now* expressed, that Haman cannot prevail against one who is of the seed of the Jews, is not *wholly* superstitious. Indeed it is a perfectly rational and devout belief when held for its own proper reasons.   But as held *by them*, it was almost purely superstitious.   They evidently thought, for a while, that this man had got the upper hand of the Jewish people, and of everything that might be called the Jewish providence. And now in an hour all is changed, and the God of the Jews, and they as His favoured people are, in their judgment, invincible. But why did they not call this to mind before, so far, at least, as to warn their master against rash and impious opposition to them, and against the framing of that inhuman edict for their destruction ?

Still, although we may despise the wife and the friends, we cannot say that by their counsel now they do Haman any injustice. They do *not* render him the highest service. The highest service would be to tell him the truth, and help him to conform to it by con-fession, repentance, and amendment.   (If they had been even worldly wise, they would have told him at once to take down the gallows.) But they do him no injustice.   The poor man (for now pity begins to rise) has been sowing diligently, and he is now to reap *as* he has sown. Black harvest comes in a day. It begins to come in his own house. There —where he had plotted the mischief, begins to fall the shadow of doom.

Yet, let us not overdraw the picture; possibly, if we knew all, there are softer lines to put into it, and some lights of human kindness. There is always much untold and unknown in these histories. Did they follow up their confident prediction that he could not succeed against Mordecai and the Jews, by earnest friendly counsel to Haman to conceal himself, or at once to take flight out of the Empire, or away to some distant part of it? We know not. We know only that they were still talking with him—talking over the whole matter—the gathering dangers, the possible methods of relief—when the conference is interrupted by the entrance of the king's chamberlains, who have come, in haste, to bring Haman to the banquet that Esther had again prepared.

That banquet, when they have come to it, is the banquet of yesterday repeated, exactly. Outwardly the scene is the same without any change—the same room or·hall! the same royal couches! Haman's rich mat spread on the floor! the lords in waiting, the obsequious attendants! The feast too is the same. But how changed is one of the company! Inwardly how much changed! Outwardly, perhaps *not* much, for he had the power of hiding and repressing feeling, and he would still *hope*, no doubt, to work himself by his great skill out of the danger. He had no idea that it was so tremendous, that it was so near! He knew not—even the king did not know—that the queen was a Jewess, and that in the vile plot which he had hatched he had made the king sign away his own queen's life.

The feast goes on as yesterday, and about the same time in the evening, perhaps a little sooner, for the king, after the sleepless night, and what has come of it to Mordecai, is eager and anxious, and fully resolved to fathom without further delay what mystery there might be in the queen's silence. He puts once more the question of yesterday, and in the same words, " What is thy petition, Queen Esther ? and it shall be granted thee ; and what is thy request ? and it shall be performed, even to the half of the kingdom."

M

It may well be that for a moment the shadow of fear fell upon the queen's heart; but in the next moment it was gone, and she spake, briefly, but clearly, and, no doubt, with the earnestness and intensity befitting the case. "Let my life be given me at my petition, and my people at my request; for we are sold—not for bondmen and bond-women, for that I had held my tongue, and even, if need were, gone with my people into slavery—but sold to black death—to be destroyed, to be slain, to perish!" Rapidly the thoughts pass through the king's mind. Even while the queen is yet speaking he is thinking:—"Sold to death? *Thy* people, and *thou*, my queen, nearer to me and dearer than any other? The sword that hangs thus over thee must hang also over me. If *thy* life is sold, can mine be safe?" And then in kingly wrath he speaks. "Who is he, and where is he, that durst presume in his heart to do so?" And then the queen—"The adversary and enemy is this wicked Haman!" Now the arrow has sped to the mark, and, quivering through Haman's inmost sensibili-ties, lies deep infixed in his heart. "He was

afraid before the king and the queen."
Apparently he manifested his fear—perhaps
stood trembling before them.   Very cruel
people are sometimes very cowardly.   Judge
Jeffreys could go through his black assize in
the West of England, the terror of the land,
manifesting the fury of a wild beast; but when
the tide turned, and he saw nothing before
him but ignominy and disgrace, he sank into
a state of abject fear which was pitiable to
see.   " Haman was afraid before the king and
the queen !"   As he well may be.   It is an
awful moment.   His life trembles in the
balance.   If the king keeps his couch he may
be spared.   If he rises up abruptly, and with-
draws, he is doomed.   The king's retirement
is like passing solemn judgment.   The custom has descended to our times, and the
Shah of Persia—the modern Ahasuerus—or
if not he, certainly some of his immediate
predecessors have condemned men to death
in this way.   " Then the king, arising from
the banquet of wine in his wrath, went into
the palace garden."   Haman ! thou art gone !
No earthly power can save thee now unless
it be that of the queen.   True, it is by her

means that the judgment has come, and come
so swiftly; but she is a woman. She will
have mercy! Now that the danger is rolled
away from herself, and probably is about to
be rolled away from her people, she may pity
even the originator of the intended tragedy.
As the king arises from his golden couch
Haman also springs up from his mat on the
floor, and stands up to make request for his
life to the queen. Skin for skin; all that a
man hath will he give for his life—his manliness, his courage, his very shame! What a
picture of terror and misery! With pallid
face, and bloodless lips, and trembling knees,
and supplicating gesture, he entreats his life;
and then in the agony of his passion he falls
on his knees, stretching out his beseeching
hands towards the queen's couch, when the
king returning at that moment from the
garden into the house, still wrathful, it would
seem almost *more* indignant than when he
went out, the fire of his rage burning the
more hotly the more he mused on the circumstances of the case—returning now at the
moment when Haman threw himself at the
queen's feet, he was inflamed still more by

beholding him. Not that he *really* thought
him guilty in what it suited his object to
impute to him ; but he evidently wished now
to hasten the end. The officers would have
covered his face when the king rose and went
into the garden, for that was the signal of
evil *determined*. It was like the black cap in
which the judge pronounces sentence of
death. But they waited to see whether the
queen would intercede for the sparing of his
life. There is no more hope now. They
cover his face, and wait the king's pleasure.

One of the chamberlains, Harbonah, stood
by. He had been to Haman's house not
more than two hours ago to fetch him to the
banquet. He had there seen the gallows, or
cross, fifty cubits high, prepared and standing
ready for Mordecai. It was perhaps in some
degree natural therefore that he should mention the circumstance. But how like the
true courtier he is, whose business it is to
shift and set the sails to all the changes of
the wind—to comply with the king's mood
to whatever it may tend. Says an old com-
mentator, "If Harbonah spake this out of
hatred of Haman's insolency, and in favour

of Mordecai's innocency and loyalty, he deserved commendation." Well, no, we think not. Hardly on any supposition does this suggestion of his look well. It is impossible to make it much less than mean. It had been better for thee, Harbonah, to have kept silence that day. For now thou hast made thyself known in history to all time as a helper of the hangman. "Nothing can be more fit," said the king; "hang him thereon." "So they hanged Haman on the gallows," or cross, "that he had prepared for Mordecai, and the king's wrath was pacified."

Now again we shall try to set forth in distinctness some of the moral instruction contained in the passage, and some of the more express lessons, just as they emerge in the narrative.

I.

We see the great importance of capable and prudent management of things. Esther's management of these great affairs is evidently consummate. She is acting no doubt throughout under Mordecai's advice—better still, she

is surely, more or less consciously, under the
infallible guidance of the good providence of
God.   But these things do not supersede her
own thought.   This woman is, in the human
sense, acting out her own plan; and from the
great results, we see how exceedingly wise
and well arranged it had been.   It is chiefly
by the results that we make this judgment.
I question if the plan itself in all its parts,
even now, commends itself to *our* prudential
judgment.   Nine persons out of ten would
say, "When Esther tells the king, let Haman
be absent."   To tell him in his presence,
after having made special provision that he
should be present, is a bolder, grander policy
perhaps ; but it is more critical, and depends
more on *every* thing being done at the right
time, and in the right temper.   Yet, as the
result proves, it is the best ; and the best is
chosen, and steadily adhered to.   We are
bound always to take the *best* plan—the best
plan of life on the whole, as far as it may lie
within our own choice ; the best course
through each separate scene ; the best way
of doing each several duty.   We have no
right to act in an aimless and indolent man-

ner, and then expect all our negligences and
slips to be made up and corrected by an
overruling providence. There *is* an overruling providence, but there is also a teaching
wisdom of God, and if we wish to be fully
under the protections of the one, we must
open all our faculties to receive the instructions of the other.

II.

We have in Esther's behaviour a very
notable and noble instance of calm and
courageous action in strict conformity with
the predetermined plan. How few women
are born into the world who *could* go through
these scenes as Esther does! How many
would faint through fear! How many would
be carried by excitement into a premature
disclosure of the secret! How many would
be under continual temptation to change the
plan! Only a select few can be calm and
strong in critical circumstances, patient and
yet intense, prudent and yet *resolved*. Her
action furnishes what it is usual now to call
a model, after which we all, and especially

good women, may strive.   Esther is by no
means, in our view, the ideal woman on the
whole.   There are finer women sketched in
Scripture than she, and far finer are imagin-
able.   But hardly anything finer is conceiv-
able than the admirable balance and adjust-
ment of various qualities in this great historical
scene.   Her behaviour is quite a study, and
conformity to it—in the spirit of course, and
not in the letter merely—ought to take us
so far towards human perfection.

III.

One thing more we must notice.   Her
boldness takes here a form which it has not
before assumed : it is shown in the denunciation of a particular person : " The adversary
and enemy is this wicked Haman."   Strong
language ; but, at any rate, it is open and
honest, and above-board—no whispering into
the king's private ear ; no secret plotting to
supplant the Prime Minister.   Every word is
uttered in the man's hearing, and to his face.
Let him deny, if he can ; let him explain, if
he can.   Let him answer.   This much cour-

tesy and justice is shown even to a notoriously bad man, and in the old heathen time. Then, surely, no Christian will ever strike at other Christians in the dark, whisper against a neighbour's reputation, set suspicions afloat which he himself has no power to recall, and which, although in some instances they may be harmless, because those against whom they are directed may be strong enough to throw them off, yet, in other instances, may do irreparable injury. But the deepest injury of all is done to the manhood, the conscience, to the sensibility, the self-respect, of those who fall into such dark ways. I would a thousand and a thousand times rather be the sufferer in such slanders than the perpetrator of them. Here is our law: "Let all bitterness, and wrath, and anger, and clamour, and evil-speaking, be put away from you, with all malice" (Paul). "Wherefore, laying aside all malice, and all guile, and hypocrisies, and envies, and all evil-speakings, as new-born babes desire the sincere milk of the word, that ye may grow thereby" (Peter).

It is not to be denied, however, that strong words do need sometimes to be spoken, even

by Christians, to each other, or by one man
to another. And here, in Esther's denunciation of Haman to his face, we have what I
find some of the commentators regard as a
good instance of courageous faithfulness which
we shall do well to imitate. Yes, in the like
circumstances, if ever we are placed in them.
But how seldom is that likely to be! If a
man is, like Haman, rapacious, perfidious,
cruel, malignant, inhuman, he may be personally denounced. But, happily, such mon-
sters are rare; while it is by no means rare
to find wrong-doing among men who stand
in various relations to each other. Now, in
regard to the treatment of all such matters
on which there may be differences of opinion
among men equally sincere, in which men
may make mistakes in action without any conscious inward swerving in principle, Esther's
example is *not* to be followed. It is not
suitable to the case. Whatever seems wrong
to any Christian conscience (every man, of
course, guided by the light of *his own* conscience) ought to be called what it seems.
It is a spurious charity that would throw a
mantle over wrong. Christians must be told

of their faults, like other people—even more than other people.

But in all ordinary instances and circumstances the *only* safe rule is this—to point out clearly and faithfully the error or the wrong (*i.e.* the things which *seem* so to the person pointing them out), but to abstain religiously not only from personal denunciation, but from judgments of personal character even, and from any intrusion into the realm of motive, into which only the eye of Omniscience can look. Surely, Christian brethren, there is a very clear distinction between those two things— between describing and condemning, it may be in strong language even, what seems to us wrong and mischievous in action, and taking a living man and putting him into our scales, that we may try and tell out the weight of his character. The one of those things we *can* do ; the other we can not do, and it can only injure us to try to do it. There are some things which I could safely and confidently describe in very strong language as inexpressibly mean and cowardly ; but I shouldn't like to permit myself to think, even to myself, none but myself knowing the thought, that

those who do such things are mean and
cowardly persons through and through —
rather I am bound to think that they may
have done wrong without consideration, as
one who scatters firebrands and says, "Am
not I in sport?" or from a misguided generous impulse, or through misinformation, and
that deep regret may come some day and fill
their hearts with sorrow.   In one word, I am
bound to hold fast in all fortunes and at all
hazards that heavenly charity which "beareth
all things, believeth all things, hopeth all
things, endureth all things."

IV.

Well, if we are to think so charitably of
the living, and make every generous supposition, and every possible allowance with a view
to any just modification of their guilt, even
when, as in some few instances, we are haunted
by the idea that they are really very bad
people, and that their whole conduct and
character are without excuse—if still, I say,
our only true and safe rule is the rule of
charity—then what about the dead?   What

about bad men when they die? What about
this sad Haman? The question is quite per-
tinent; for here is the mortal part of him,
hanging, as it were, in our sight, not taken
down from the gallows yet. Where has the
inner, real Haman gone—the dark, proud,
active, malignant, implacable spirit that ani-
mated the now tenantless clay? What has
become of him; what is he doing, suffering,
dreading? The real answer to these questions, and to all such like questions, if we
would be perfectly honest with ourselves, is
this: We do not know. We know so far, and
then comes the mystery and the darkness
through which we see not. That such a man
can have gone to heaven,—that is impossible;
unless we are to believe that God governs the
world and the universe insincerely, and by
freaks of moral despotism and surprise. That
he has gone to hell would seem to be certain;
and chiefly for this reason, that he has taken
hell with him. The unsubdued will, the reck-
less ambition, the pride that scorches every
gentle thing within the heart where it dwells,
the hatred that *burns* where it throbs: how
can a man but be in hell with such things as

these in the breast—the earth having slipped
away from under him, her pleasures, her dignities, her pursuits, her changes, all over and
gone ?

But—but, if to the living Haman, bad as
he is or seems, utterly, we are to be—while
hating and condemning and denouncing his
bad actions and his bad inner qualities as far
as they are displayed—if we are yet to be,
what God is to us all, charitable and merciful,
then surely we are not to be less so to the
man when he is dead.

He has died, and made, not any meritorious
atonement, but in the natural sense he has
paid the price and made atonement to society
for the evil of his life. Then his dead form
shall be as sacred to me as if it lay in a coffin
wrapt in a costly winding-sheet, and anointed
with sweet spices, while friends stand weeping
beside the bier. If there be none to weep
to-day, if his friends have all fled away in
shame or terror, there is the less need for my
scorn or condemnation; there is the more need
for what reverence I can feel in the presence
of death, for what pity I can legitimately
cherish for one who must have had a great

inheritance of natural ability and yet has brought it all to this shipwreck of an untimely end. *He has died* thus in disgrace and shame ; he who might have lived so well ! What *might* have been—ah! what might have been ? It will do us good to think of it for a moment. That dark but intellectual face *might* have worn the smiles of benevolence ; those fingers which wrote death-edicts to spread terror through the land, and gathered and clutched at the gold and silver as though man's eternal happiness lay in them, *might* have been busy these many years in writings and labours of helpful kindness to a whole kingdom ; and that heart that has just ceased to beat, or rather the spiritual heart within, might have given pulse and sway to many a noble purpose. It might have been ; it might have been ! A great preacher of the sixteenth century, who became martyr in the reign of Mary, used to say as he saw the hurdle pass bearing some poor doomed wretch to Tyburn, " There goes John Bradford (himself) but for the grace of God !" Yes, standing beside the saintliest death-bed one may profitably think how these feet, which are about to walk on

the high places of heaven, *might* have slipped
and gone the other way; and, standing beside
the darkest cross, one may think how the poor
outcast who hangs on it, detected, scorned,
and crucified, *might* have had the saintliest
death, and been crowned with glory, honour,
and immortality. " Let him that thinketh he
standeth take heed lest he fall ;" and let him
that standeth in grace beside one who *has*
fallen be gentle, and merciful, and leave all
judgment to the righteous and ever-merciful
God.

But is not this something like tampering
with moral distinctions ? No. Not in the
least. The dark lessons of Haman's life remain the same. This man is taken in red-
handed guilt. He is caught in the net he was
spreading, falls into the pit his own hands had
dug, and deserves to die as clearly as any one
ever did, if violent death by law is justifi-
able at all. And who can but see in his fall
the punishment of pride, the mockery of unprincipled ambition, the home-coming swing
of malignant schemes intended to injure
others ? Who can fail to see the futility of
race-hatreds—such as hatred of Russians or

N

hatred of Turks—and how God in his providence often works against such hatreds and
defeats them, giving *every* people some opportunity and chance, even as every man ? Who
can fail to see that the doom of a wicked
and cruel selfishness, like that of Haman, is
a black and bitter doom when it comes ? The
moral lessons from such a life are clear
enough, and incontestible. And we can have
them all without parting from those sweet
companions, gentle pity and heavenly charity.
Above all, we surely are able to read and
learn such lessons as these, without encroach-
ing on divine prerogative, without professing
a belief in things which God has not revealed,
and which, even intellectually, we cannot
fully comprehend.

" If thine enemy hunger, feed him. If
he thirst, give him drink,"—and if, by the
laws of society he must be hanged, at least
by no human mortal lips let him be damned.
Leave him to the judgments of the Holy
One. Leave him to the mercies of the All-
Merciful.

V.

You all know what far other associations we have with a cross. You know how this symbol of guilt and shame has been changed and glorified, so as symbol never was before. Mordecai had the cross erected for him but he escaped it, and Haman himself had to enact the part.

The great "Adversary," the Haman of all ages and all countries, plotted with evil men for the death of the righteous One, and He accepted the issue. He died on the cross, that He might be able to save all men with crucified reputations, and crucified hearts, sinners whom no one would pity or touch.

Ah, but you say the devil at least gained the outward triumph? Yes, but no more than outward. Christ made the cross really a throne of glory and a chariot of triumph. Satan himself was overcome and spiritually crucified in and by the cross he had raised for Jesus. "By death Christ destroyed him that had the power of death, that is the devil, and delivered them who through fear of death were all their lifetime subject to bondage."

LECTURE IX.

CHAPTER VIII., Verses i. to vii.

ESTHER GOING IN TO THE KING TO MAKE REQUEST FOR HER PEOPLE.

"THE evil that men do lives after them." That is certain, whether or no it be true that "the good is oft interred with their bones." The *particular* evil which Haman had wrought during the time that has passed before us in this history could hardly be said to be made any less by his own departure out of the world. It lay, as we know, in a diabolical plot for the destruction of a whole people, which he had hatched in his own dark brain and malignant heart, and to which, in an evil hour, by his persuasive acts, he had obtained the king's consent and seal. It would almost appear that the king did not really know what he was doing. In some cunning way the case in its bare and dreadful reality was kept from his knowledge—else how could he with so much indignation and surprise exclaim when Esther reveals to him the deadly plot, "Who is he, and where is he, that durst presume in his heart to do so?" Well, he who presumed in his heart to do so has met the reward of his deeds now, and has gone to his own place; but his deeds remain; and especially the chief deed of his last days remains, in such a form, that if nothing be done for the abolition or the counteraction of the deadly edict, there will be such scenes of terror and blood, such massacre and murder throughout the Empire, wrought upon an innocent and defenceless people, as will be almost enough to give Haman a sense of revenge in his grave! Now let us see what in these circumstances was done by the king, by Mordecai, by Esther; and how the character of each comes out in what they did.

I.

What the king did. When a traitor or a great culprit like Haman dies, he forfeits all his estates and possessions to the crown. This has been the law in nearly every country, and was likely to be so in its most rigorous form in Persia. It is a hard rough law, and, quite possibly, at least in certain instances, it is full of injustice and unkindness to the children. *They* might be loyal, and patriotic, and humane. But no chance is given them. The shadow of the cross must darken Haman's home for ever, *i.e.* as long as it is a home. Those who have not sinned must suffer. Nay—as has often happened here in England, as elsewhere, the children of fathers who suffered—not for doing wrong, but for doing nobly, have the stigma put upon them by the despotic authority, just as if they themselves had done wrong. This race-law, as applied by men, is terrible.

Well, the first thing the king did (and it was done promptly, on the very day of Haman's death) was to " give the house of Haman, the Jews' enemy, to Esther the queen."

" The house of Haman " means all that he had. He had talked to his wife and his friends of " the glory of his riches," which must therefore have been great. They are all handed over in royal gift to Esther. And " the ring " which Haman had worn, which the king had presented to him—taking it from his own royal hand to do so, and which had been taken from Haman before his death, by the chamberlain, and brought again to the king—that ring the king again took from his royal hand, and presented it, this time to a worthier custodian—to Mordecai, who had already saved his life, and who has been all through this business displaying a silent but masterly ability in the management of affairs. On this account, and also because the queen just at this juncture revealed to the king the relationship existing between Mordecai and herself—Mordecai " came before the king." He came evidently because he was sent for. The king has been told now of all his kindness to the orphan girl left in his care ; how he has brought her up as his own child ; how he has sanctioned and advised all the steps she has taken in her life. The king himself knows, and would remember with a new vividness at this time, how he had been beholden to him for his own life, which, but for Mordecai's intelligence and fidelity, would have been sacrificed in a plot to the wrath of Bigthan and Teresh, the two chamberlains. The king thinks:—He is able: he is faithful: he has had experience: he is calm and brave and not to be turned aside from the path of duty: he is closely related to the queen, who has acted so worthily of her great rank and office: and who, apart from her own love to me, which seems to be most sincere, *can* have no motive to seek anything but my safety and the welfare of the Empire. Who then so fit to wear the chief dignity, to fill the vacant office, to lift and use the suspended power—as he? " Mordecai, I promote thee, as I promoted Haman the son of Hammedetha the Agagite. I advance thee as I advanced him; and set thy seat, as I set his seat, above all the princes. And all my servants shall bow before thee and do thee reverence. Be my prime minister; and take the ring which will be the visible symbol to others of the honour and of the office to

which thou art now raised." The forfeited
estate to Esther—the vacant office to Mordecai—to the one the riches, and what glory
may come with them!—to the other, the
power and what good uses may be made
of it.

And so the king has done his part, and
has done it royally, and *like* a king. And it
does not seem to strike him that there is anything else to do. It is so easy for kings,
without being wicked or tyrannical, and for
those in high social rank, without being of
evil disposition, to take only *the grand* view
of things, or the view that naturally and
habitually presents itself to them, and to forget
altogether, or perhaps never even really know,
what common life is, and what the needs
are, and what the thoughts, and what the
dangers, of the great masses of their fellow-
creatures who are living and dying around
them. Then *is* this all thou hast to do, O
king, in the present emergency, and as responsible to the King of kings? Hast thou
forgotten that night, not so long ago, when
" the king and Haman sat down to drink,"
while "perplexity" prevailed in the city

around them, and " the posts," hastened by
the king's commandment, sped on to far
provinces, weighted with the black message of
death. Hast thou never, on *any* day since
then, thought for one serious moment of the
horror and consternation which would seize
on the Jewish communities of the different
cities when the heavy tidings came to them?
Hast thou never pictured, in imagination, the
anguish of the Jewish household, and the
silent misery of individual hearts—fathers
looking ruthfully upon stalwart sons, mothers
clasping doomed infants and little children to
their breasts? Nay; these are not thoughts
for a king! they are not thoughts, at least,
for a king like thee. Thou canst be in a
rage at wickedness which thine own hand
hath wrought. Thou canst hang thy partner
in the crime on his cross of shame, divesting
him of all his dignities and wealth. Having
offered such a sacrifice to justice, thou canst
deign to let it be known, so that it may be
chronicled to all ages that ' the king's wrath
is pacified,' and then thou canst distribute
gift, and largess, and honour, and power, to
thy queen and thy new prime minister, and

then, after banqueting, thou canst go to thy kingly couch, for what one knows, with the quiet mind of one who thinks he has done virtuously, and in the records of the empire it may somewhere be written, 'On that night *could* the king sleep—soundly and well, and next morning he awoke refreshed.'

So much for the king and his part in this crisis of affairs.

II.

Now let us look at what is done by Mordecai. As far as the words of the passage go, he seems to do little or nothing—nothing actively; he *seems* entirely passive. But this is far from being the case. He is a silent man, and unobtrusive. He seems to have no ambitions, except such as would advance the interests of his own countrymen while not injuring those of the country in which he dwells; but he is sleeplessly vigilant concerning all that is taking place, and in quiet, unseen ways is really directing, as far as one man may, the whole course of the history.

If it be said that there is no sufficient
evidence of this in the narrative, the answer
is, that evidence to this effect is all summed
up in the simple fact of his appointment to
the premiership of the greatest country in the
world. This king is vain, and proud, and
selfish, and heartless—but he is not a fool.
And it would be folly of the highest and
most mischievous kind to put an incompetent
stranger at the head of his vast affairs.
Some way or other Mordecai has shown, and
the king has noted, his possession of the
qualities that fit him for the great place. In
these all-important transactions, as it seems
to us, Mordecai is the chief power, although
Esther is the chief actor. We do not hint
that she hath not her own full share of merit,
and that share a large one. But it seems to
us all but certain that, in all her actions and
behaviour at this time, she is carrying out
the plan of another—her foster-father, her
friend beyond all friends. As we read the
verses we cannot but feel his firm, silent
presence. No doubt it is he who decides at
what time Esther shall make known to the
king his, Mordecai's, relationship to her.

" To everything there is *a season*, and *a time* to every purpose under the heavens." To do a thing, a good thing, at the wrong time, is sometimes worse than not doing it at all. If it is done too soon—the evil powers have warning, opposing currents set in, and head winds blow in the face of the good purpose, and effort is in vain. If it is done too late, then—although perhaps there are no contrary winds, no strong currents to be stemmed, the silent tide of time and circumstance has turned, and the vessel of your purpose must go with it. If Esther had declared the secret sooner, Haman would have known it, and *might* have found some diabolical means of destroying even the queen herself and all the Jews. If she had declared it later, some one else, meantime, might have got the ring of office instead of Mordecai, for, as we have already said, his relationship to the queen certainly seems to have been *one* reason for his appointment, and was probably even the deciding one.

Yes, " to everything there is a season, and a time to every purpose under the heavens :" a time to keep silence, and a time to speak.

One says that " He that would be able to speak *when* and *as* he ought, must first learn silence as the Pythagoreans did of old." St. Jerome saith, " Let us first learn *not* to speak, that afterwards we may open our mouths to speak wisely." Some one gives this as a rule :—" Either keep silence, or give that which is better than silence." It need not be always supreme wisdom, or profound truth, to be better than silence. After all, our tongues have been given us at least for occasional speech. The word of kindness is good. The word of sympathy—even the smallest word will be helpful if it comes in the right time. But oh! how important is it in the great matters of life to speak in the right time as Esther did! and how all-important that we should speak to the great King asking His grace while yet it is the day of grace. Blessed be His name, this is heaven's " time " and " season " for all men. " Now ! " now is the accepted time. " Now "—the tide is full, but still flowing : turn your vessel, and glide over the bar while you may. " Now "—the gale is blowing gently and favourably; spread the sail of your purpose, and catch its favouring breath, and haste away from breaker and sandbank over the quiet seas to the realms of sunshine. "Now"—the drawbridge is down—enter the castle of safety. "Now" —the door is open. Come in—for in no long time a voice from within will say to those who come knocking, "The door is shut!"

Now let us see the hand of this silent masterful man in another thing—another thing of "time and season." There can be little doubt that it is he who decides, or at any rate strongly suggests, that Esther shall *again* go in before the king as a suppliant to plead for her people. That the thought never entered her mind until it was suggested, it would be too much to say. Succeeding so well in her first endeavour, it would be every way natural for her to think of renewing it on behalf of her people. But the right time for doing so, we may be sure, would be fixed by Mordecai, at any rate in consultation with him. It is he who has the threads of the plan in his hand. It is he who has the justly deliberating judgment, the accurately forecasting eye, the patient temper, the unswerving will,

the ready hand, the silent tongue which grows
eloquent now and again only for the moment
when he has to say, "*Now !*"   "Do it now."

III.

Let Mordecai now retire for a little into
his congenial shade, while Esther comes forward, and ventures, as before, into the kingly
presence to ask, if she is allowed, the reversal
of the edict against the Jews.   The account
of the queen's entrance is more brief than on
the occasion of her former appearance.   No
doubt, however, the form of the thing would
be much the same.   The king would be on
the throne or seat of dignity for the consideration and transaction of public affairs.
Esther's matter is not a thing to be talked
over in private between king and queen.   It
is a thing which, alas ! has gone irrevocably
into public law, and must be publicly regarded and settled.   The king on the throne,
Esther, too, as before, would come in arrayed
in royal apparel, or "in her royalty," looking
her best—queenly in face and movement,
making no attempt to trick herself out in

meretricious charms, which one easily sup-
poses she knew she didn't need, but trusting
to the graces which never fail—simplicity,
modesty, dignity, directness, and attended, no
doubt, as a quaint old author says she was in
the former case, not by two maids, as Josephus
hath it, but by those three faithful companions, Faith, Hope, and Charity, who
brought her off also with safety.

There are, however, differences between
this and her former audience well worthy of
being noted. On the first occasion *she stood.*
When the king saw her *standing* in the inner
court, immediately he held out the golden
sceptre. *Now* she falls down at his feet, and
beseeches him " *with tears* to put away the
mischief of Haman, the Agagite." The prostrate attitude of the queen now is assumed
to express the utmost lowliness and humility;
but at the same time it seems to express a
growing confidence in the king's clemency,
and possibly, also, a growing inward conviction of her own influence over him, partly by
her own means and partly by the power and
character of him who now holds the great seal.
Yet the confidence is by no means complete,

O

else why should the " tears" come so quickly
from their fountains ?   If she knew that what
she asks would be got simply for the asking,
there would be no tears ; there would be
hardly even the falling down at the king's
feet.   No ; the request *may* be denied ; the
proud monarch may be unwilling to confess
himself mistaken and fallible, in his former
action.   There may be legal difficulties in
setting edict against edict in a country where
the law is that no duly-enacted law can be
reversed.   The clear reversal of the law she
knows she need not seek.   Any enactment
coming short of this, and yet capable of
bringing something like the same effect, must
be difficult to find, and perhaps not easy
safely to promulgate.   Therefore, with a pas-
sionate earnestness, bending at his feet, looking, perhaps, timidly yet pathetically and im-
ploringly into his face ; weeping while she
speaks, yet continuing to speak while she
weeps ; touchingly, terribly different from the
queen he has never seen before except in her
smiles or in her grandeur, yet somehow fairer
in his eyes, and dearer to his better heart in
this burst of tragic eagerness, in this passion

of unselfish grief, than when queening it in splendour with the king and Haman for guests ; so she pleads, and he listens for a few moments. He could not listen long. He feels at once that this is a battle that must quickly come to an end. A rain of hot fire like this he has never been subject to before. Whatever is done must be done *quickly*, and what shall it be ? In a dark fitful breast like his some sudden gust of anger may arise. Annoyed by being reminded, although only delicately and incidentally, of his own share in the fabrication of the edict of horror, and fearful of plots from the other side by too much favour shown to these Jews, he may say, " Much as I have loved thee, O queen ! thou hast presumed to come forbidden into my presence once too often ; thou shalt be taken from it now—to die !" This was quite possible. He did not require, indeed, to do or say anything to bring this terrible issue. If he remained impassive—simply *not* holding out the golden sceptre—those who covered Haman's face were not far away, and their supple, obsequious, ignominious hands were ready, at the signal, to put a thicker veil over

Esther's face than that made by her own escaping tresses, and to lead her quickly to her doom.

But no; "the king held out the golden sceptre towards Esther," and the danger is past as far as it affects herself; and with a little more perseverance the safety of her people also will be secured. The king held out the golden sceptre, and the queen arose. She had "humbled herself under the mighty hand of God," as well as before her earthly lord, and lo! she is exalted in due season. Never is the moon so beautiful as when she escapes from the thick bank of envious cloud which lay dark against her rising, and sails into the clear blue of the open sky. "So Esther arose and stood before the king;" stood, no doubt, as before, in her royalty, although probably with lessening sense of it in her own breast. She is thinking, now increasingly and intensely, of the one all-important cause of her being here at all. She is thinking, perhaps, "Twice my life has been spared, yet soon it will not be worth keeping if I cannot save the life of my people." "So Esther arose and stood before the king;" and either asked by him as before, "What is thy petition, and what is thy request ?" or, receiving some sign that she may speak, immediately begins to plead.

The pleading is very skilful. In form it is simple and inartistic, and apparently irregular, yet in substance it would not be easy to imagine a wiser or better putting of the case. The fair advocate is full of self-deprecation and self-distrust, and at the same time renders ample reverence and honour to the king and to the law. She seems almost to hesitate as she speaks, almost to withdraw one phrase that she may put the next in the stead of it, if possibly it may be happier. "If it please the king !" Nothing can be done against the king's good pleasure. "And if I have found favour in his sight." If the poor advocate is not altogether unworthy of the cause she is venturing to plead. "And the thing seem *right* before the king ;" who, no doubt, will do not only what pleases him, but what seems " right" and best, guiding himself by many royal considerations of which I, a woman, must be ignorant. "And I be pleasing in his sight"—"if it please the king ;" " and if I have found favour in his sight;" "and the thing seem right before the king;" "and if I be pleasing in his sight!" Ah! Queen Esther, we would not, after the noble things we have seen in thee, and are yet to see, hastily or easily impute to thee any insincerity of speech or behaviour; but surely thou hast some faint, flitting idea, if not in thy queenly conscious-ness, yet in thy deeper woman's heart, that thou *art*—shall we say just *a little?*—pleas-ing to the king. Art thou altogether desti-tute of a shrewd suspicion that it is the king's pleasure in thee that has turned the scale once and again in moments of tremendous crisis; and that, in fact, while indebted to Mordecai for foresight, plan, direction, yet that, single-handed thou hast been fighting this battle, and art now well nigh finally winning it by thy courage, thy beauty, and thy tears?

The climax of the queen's earnest, appeal-ing prayer is reached in the 6th verse. There is in it just perhaps a touch of the self-con-sciousness of which we have spoken: "If I be pleasing in the king's eyes, then let him see to this matter without delay. All the king's pleasure in me, as queen, will end assuredly with the falling of this judgment, if it is permitted to fall. If my people die, I must die with them. I cannot endure to see their destruction." The feeling thus begins, perhaps, in some little self-consciousness, but it ends sublimely in self-sacrifice. She realises to the full the terrible danger in which they stand, the silent agony in which they are waiting, even now, not knowing if any relief can be found ; and she flings herself thus, with all the dignities and pleasures of her life, in sincere self-abandonment, with a patriotic affection as tender as it is strong, between them and death. And the sacrifice is effectual, and the prayer is heard and answered without the least delay.

O queen, thou art victor now! Thou art ascending a higher and a holier throne than that on which thou wast crowned on the day of thine espousals. Thy great king was but now holding forth to thee the golden sceptre on which thy very life was hung, and thou didst arise and stand as a weeping suppliant before him. And lo! now thou art waving a far more powerful sceptre, albeit invisible, over his head! Thou art ruling him partly by the power of womanly beauty and accomplishment over a fitful but susceptible nature, but still more by the irresistible power of moral earnestness, by the grandeur of patriotism, and by the holy spell of self-sacrificing love! And soon the pens of the scribes will be busy for thee, and the swift beasts will be carrying thy message of life to distant provinces, and thy poor people far and near will gratefully bless thy name.

In our humble judgment, this is the sublimest part in Esther's life, as far as we know it. This in which, having secured the safety of her own life, she does not "count it dear to herself," but ventures it all *again* in an act of uncalculating self-sacrifice, telling the king that what he has already given is of no value to her unless he will also give the life of her people.

Indeed there is no sublimity of human character to equal that which is reached in such a mood. Take the greatest men who have lived, in their greatest moments, you will find that either they are in this mood or in one not far removed from it. Morally, the grandest act in the life of Moses, to our thinking, is not to be found on the granite peaks of Sinai amid the thunders, and the darkness, and the flames ; nor on Pisgah, with the far-stretching land of promise lying in light before him ; but when grieved, and humbled, and disappointed with the idolatries of the people, and yet clinging passionately to them still, he threw himself before God as their intercessor, crying, " Oh, this people have sinned a great sin ; yet now, if thou wilt forgive their sin,—and if not, blot me, I pray Thee, out of Thy book which Thou hast written." If I fail in this, I fail in every-thing. Life itself will hardly be desirable any longer. If this people for whom I have lived is to die, let me die with them, and let us all be forgotten together.

David could sing with loud voice to the praise of God. He could cry to Him in the lonely wilderness, by night, until his voice echoed among the rocks and hills. He could fight at the head of the bravest. He could sometimes magnanimously spare the life of an enemy, even when, by sacrificing that life, his own advancement would be promoted. But among all the moods of his life, none, probably, is really diviner than that which is expressed in these words, written apparently while his heart was melted, while his tears were flowing—"Rivers of waters run down mine eyes, because they keep not Thy law."

St. Paul, often great in this greatness, is never more conspicuously so than when he declares that he has "great heaviness and continual sorrow in his heart," and that he "could wish that himself were accursed from Christ, for his brethren, his kinsmen according to the flesh." Like Esther, his cry is, "How can I endure to see the destruction of my kindred?"—only his meaning covers the spiritual and the eternal, Esther's only affecting this time-life.

But the *really perfectly sublime* of this condition or state is found only in the Master, who not only wished and desired the good of all, and lived promoting it, but actually died for us; gave life for life, the just for the unjust—redeemed us from the curse of the law by being made a curse for us. Oh for a love of race-kindred like that of Esther; for a love of country like that of David; for a love of souls like that of Christ!

Now observe, in conclusion, that the principles of noble action, and the affections, and resolutions, and preferences corresponding to them, are the same to us as they were to Esther, although we are not, and never look to be, in her pathetic and tragic circumstances. But these tragic scenes in her life, in any life, or in any part of history, are valuable to us, and have spell and power over us, not because they are *exceptions utterly* to all ordinary consciousness and experience of man, but because they are intensified specimens and expressions of *our* noblest and best. So we ought to be living in our daily life—in principle and spirit, in aim and purpose, in affection and desire—rising above the mere circumstances of our life, and always seeking and always finding its highest duties ; putting self down from the high place she is always ready to take ; seeking others' good not only without hypocrisy and in real sincerity, but with a passion of desire that will accept no denial, that will burn up the difficulties that stand in the way. If in our breast there lives any purpose that has been wisely formed, that has the good of others for its object—those in our family, our neighbourhood, our nation—keep we to that as to our life. It is the share we have in the life of Christ ; and, like His, is unconquerable, incorruptible, and immortal.

LECTURE X.

CHAPTER VIII. Verse 7 to the end.

JOY AND GLADNESS,

A FEAST AND A GOOD DAY.

E have come now to the chief or last turning-point in this history. We passed it at the close of the last Lecture.

When the king the second time holds out the golden sceptre to Esther, when he accepts her and yields to her plea, not only is her own life safe, for that had been given to her before, but the "life of her people," for which she had made "request," is now assured.

As far as any assurance can be given, even by the king; for here, indeed, is a terrible circumstance, that that edict of death possesses of necessity the dignity and inviolability of any, of every decree of the great

Persian Empire. It cannot be reversed in terms, yet since the practical reversal of it is the thing sought, and is the thing which, in substance and form, the king has consented to grant as far as possible, some means, of course, must be found of turning the edge of the decree, and furnishing to the Jews means of escape from it. What shall they be? The king treats the matter in his own right royal fashion. Esther and Mordecai stand before him, and he says, "Behold," as you well know, "I have given Esther the house of Haman," all the wealth he had amassed, and his forfeited estate, "and him they have hanged." He is gone for ever. As to what remains, the preservation, the safety of your people, "write ye also as it liketh you." "As it liketh you!" Don't trouble me with too many particulars. I am a monarch, not a statesman. There are scribes, there are wise men; and thou, Mordecai, art wise. "As it liketh you!" "As it liketh you;" only take care of this, that ye make no attempt to repeal that which is unrepealable, and that ye do not touch the dignity of the Empire.

Whether Mordecai took counsel with others does not appear; probably he is himself chiefly responsible for the plan adopted, for it is said that "the scribes wrote according to all that Mordecai commanded." The resolution was the only one that could be taken. Reversal of the decree being impossible, the policy of *resistance to it* must be adopted. The Jews are allowed to combine in self-defence; to defend themselves with weapons of war; to assail those who meant to attack them in the execution of the bloody decree; to assail them—not merely to parry the intended blow, but to give the death-blow to the assailants; to "destroy," "kill," "cause to perish;" to do this after the savage method of nearly all the ancient warfare, without showing mercy to women, or to children; and to take whatever spoil they might be able thus to win.

This is in brief and for substance the famous edict which Mordecai devised, and which was solemnly enacted in the king's name, and sealed with the king's ring. The decree was given with all order and solemnity at Shushan, the palace.

But to give it at Shushan, the palace, is one thing ; to have it published, and read, and known in the places where it will be most needed, is another. This great Persian Empire, remember, stretched from India to Ethiopia, and contained an hundred and twenty-seven provinces. These provinces were peopled not by one race, or by a few, but by a great many ; unto every people the royal decrees were made known in their own several language. The mere work of translation must have been one large department of the state. The foreign office at Shushan must have been at times a busy place, and no doubt the scribes and learned men were greatly respected, just as they are among ourselves now. Translated thus, and sealed with the ring in every language, the next thing is to have it conveyed with all speed and safety to these various and wide-lying places of destination. It will be a long time before it reaches some of them ; but all the best means of locomotion at that time possessed were put into use freely, and I do not know that there would be very much difference in regard to speed and certainty of travel between that time and this—I mean in that particular district of the world. The animals they rode on then for speed are the same swift and patient creatures that are used in these countries now —horses, mules, camels, young dromedaries. Nor would the Persian roads of this day be found better, if so good, as in that old time. The edict seems to have reached *every* province, without fail, and in time to enable the Jews to concert among themselves the means of defence against the day of danger when it should arrive.

The decree was given in the month Sevan, " the month of May," says an old author, " when all things are in their prime and pride, and the earth chequered and entrailed with variety of flowers, and God is seen to be *magnus in minimis*—great in the smallest creatures. Then did the Sun of righteousness arise to these afflicted exiles with healing in his wings, like as the sunbeams did to the dry and cold earth, calling out the herbs and flowers, and healing those deformities that winter had brought upon it."

When all this was done, and the edict of life and hope to the Jews was on its way to the provinces, a special honour was conferred upon Mordecai. "He went out," we read, "from the presence of the king in royal apparel of blue and white, and with a great crown of gold, and with a garment of fine linen and purple." Not long ago he had been gorgeously arrayed and led in triumphal procession through the city. That, however, was no more than a transient honour, speaking very loudly of the king's favour for the time, but *not* to be repeated. *This* investiture is intended apparently to express, not merely the high favour of the king resting on Mordecai for the time, but his appointment also permanently to the now vacant place of *first* counsellor of the king, first practical ruler of the great empire. As the people very well knew that the king did not interfere much, scarcely indeed at all, in the practical management of state affairs, and that the power really was in the hands of a very few, and most of all in the hands of the chief or prime minister, we can easily see that it was no slight thing to them when a *new* possessor of the power came out from the king's presence. On *whose* head sits this crown of

gold ? On *whose* shoulders hangs the rich
garment of fine linen and purple ? Who is
the wearer of the royal apparel of blue and
white ? These are questions of the deepest
interest for the citizens of Shushan, and for *all*
the citizens of the empire. We need not,
therefore, be surprised to be told in the same
verse that shows us Mordecai thus gorgeously
arrayed, that " the city of Shushan rejoiced
and was glad," nor to be told, in the next
verse, that " the Jews had light, and gladness,
and joy, and honour."

This is a book of contrasts. Almost every
character in the book passes from one extreme
of some kind to another. So does Mordecai.
Look at that man, at the centre of the city,
observed of all, clothed in sackcloth, ashes on
his head, casting himself on the ground in
the deepest trouble, and rending the air with
loud and bitter cries ! Look at this man
coming from the king's presence, splendid in
raiment, joyful in countenance. It is the
same man, and happily we can respect him
as much in the sackcloth as in the purple,
and as much in the purple as in the sackcloth. " Happy elevation," may we not say,

"which is thus immediately productive of
'light, and gladness, and joy, and honour' to
others." As, on the other hand, that is a
miserable advancement to any man which is
followed by jealousies, envyings, animosities,
bitter rivalries. It is not given, even to good
men, to escape these things always and
entirely. The world hated the perfect One,
and the world will not love His truest servants:
which means this essentially, that bad people
cannot love good people. But they respect
them, they fear them, and sometimes they may
be said almost to love them. As in the case before us, "many of the people of the land became
Jews ; for the fear of the Jews fell upon them."

We shall not now go farther in the story.
What remains of history can all be told in
the next Lecture. And meantime we shall
review what has passed before us, with an aim
to find any points of specific instruction
worthy of being considered by us.

I.

We can hardly fail to notice the well-
known peculiarity of the laws of the Medes

and Persians—that they must stand for ever ;
and can in no circumstances be directly
repealed ! How presumptuous, and how ex-
tremely foolish such a law or principle seems
to us now ! And yet this Persian Empire
contained, at the time, within itself, a large
part of the world's civilisation. And they
seemed quite to glory in this—that no law
once enacted could ever be repealed. We say
" *they* seemed to glory in this." But it really
is hardly likely that the body of the people
ever did. The principle looks like a court-
born thing. It probably had a king for its
nursing-father, and a queen for its nursing-
mother. It is evidently intended to illustrate
the grandeur of royalty, which seems to reach
the height of its majesty when it sets its
seal to some decree and says, " That is for
ever." " For ever !" And yet, supposing it
even to be wise and just, and adapted to the
circumstances in which, and with a view to
which, it is enacted, can anything be more
certain than this, that in no long time circumstances will be altogether changed ; and the
decree, therefore, will be altogether unwise
and inapplicable? But it must not be touched!

The truth is, we suppose, that laws in this way were often evaded. They were forgotten. They were not mentioned. They were practically repealed, as in the case we have on hand, by the enactment of statutes quite opposed in substance to them. But there can be little doubt that this principle of their law, taken in connection with the thoughts and customs that would naturally gather about it, would do its part in ruining the Persian Empire.

Soon or late, all human infallibility, so called, comes to grief. Political infallibility is not now professed anywhere in the world. No nation on the face of the earth is so foolish as to put out such a creed. Yet in these our own days there has been solemnly decreed and declared for the first time, formally at least, the infallibility of the sovereign Pontiff — the Roman Catholic Bishop of Rome. It is to superficial sight a strange phenomenon of these latter days, although there is much in the state of society, both in regard to opinion and morals, to account for it. Doubts, and uncertainties and unbeliefs, have so advanced their claims as to create some alarm in devout and thoughtful hearts, lest all certainty should vanish and all faith should die out of the world. They are neither the strongest minds nor the devoutest hearts which have had the fear : but it has prevailed — and great ecclesiastical persons, some of them perhaps sharing in some slight degree in the apprehension, have been quick to see and seize the opportunity for advancing the principle of human authority in religion by securing the declaration of the personal infallibility of the pope. That it is the principle of authority generally, the power of the priesthood in fact, which they have been promoting, is evident from two considerations at least — first that this personal infallibility has never been exercised in any one specific act or law. As a matter of fact, this is true as we believe. There has been no declared instance of the personal infallibility in regard to anything whatever. They have been con- tented to have the thing decreed and held as a general faith. Then, secondly, they have been able to enhance the urgency and per- emptoriness of their counsels and their invita- tions to a distracted world to come to the

place of true rest ; to the shadow of change-
less authority ; to the one infallibility in the
world. Nor can it be doubted that these
invitations have been welcome to some ; and
that they have been therefore to some extent
accepted. But the real effects of that decree
of infallibility have not yet begun to appear.
No human infallibility can prosper in the
end : the spiritual, perhaps, even less than
the political. The pretension is more impious.
The falsehood is more gigantic. The mischief more radical and more permanent : and
the overthrow of the principle when it comes
will be more complete. When that end is
attained, all free minds and devout hearts
will have " light and gladness, and joy and
honour." " Joy and gladness, a feast and a
good day "—among all the tribes of Israel,
and in all the provinces of the kingdom
of grace, will come when the commandment of the heavenly King, which brings
peace, and purity, and liberty, and love, is
received.

II.

There is something in all human action unrepealable. In an evil hour that black edict of death went out sealed with the king's seal. It was not to be put in execution for many long months. It is now practically revoked as far as it can be. And really, looking at the circumstances, one cannot help wondering how it was that means could not be found by the king's wise men to make it practically innocuous, to make it as though it had never been enacted — so that not one single human life should fall by its means in any way. But it couldn't be, apparently. The Jews are saved largely, but the Persians bleed. They fall in great numbers under an edict that was never intended to touch them. If the Jews' enemies, who seem to have been numerous and envenomed, had been wise and prudent, still more, if they had been charitable and fraternal, perhaps they *might* have obviated almost the whole of the bloody issue of the business that came. But the only way of making quite sure that we shall obviate or nullify the consequences of an evil action, or an evil course of conduct (if one may express the thing in a strong solecism) is—not to do the action ; not to follow the course of conduct. For when the deed is done, when the movement is on foot, when the influence is spreading, it is utterly beyond our power to arrest, and modify, and extinguish at our will. Few things are more melancholy and affecting than the deep concern and trouble of aroused consciences in view of things deeply regretted, but seen to be beyond recall, and, in a large degree, intractable to modification and management. It is easy to touch a spring in a piece of complex machinery where there is force of water or steam pent up and ready to play ; but if you don't know all the consequences, you had better *not* touch the spring. Still more, if human lives will be endangered certainly, or other serious mischief made possible, then, surely, you would restrain your hand.

We must not take a morbid view, and afflict ourselves with imaginary fears, and think of this great machine we call providence as if it were full of lurking mischiefs ready to break out at the slightest touch. It is indeed a thing of immense vitality and force. In the bosom of providence, *i.e.* in the heart of our human life here where we are living it, lie stored the influences of the past, the present interests of living men, a thousand plans, a thousand purposes, and thousands of wills, guiding them and urging them on to effectuation, and the divine power overruling all. In this great process things are perverted. Things meant for good, by touching evil things, are turned to evil; things meant for evil, on the other hand, are smitten by the royal power of goodness, and almost changed in their nature. We are not responsible for these changes. We are not responsible for all subtle combinations into which our action may be drawn with other things after it has passed from ourselves. We are responsible chiefly, almost exclusively, for this—the action in itself, the course of conduct in itself. We cannot control the consequences, and we shall not be accountable for them except in so far as they are the direct and proper fruit of the action. If we do what is right, and wise, and for good reasons, we have nothing to fear. If we do wilfully or carelessly what we know to be wrong, we have every reason to look for the evil consequences, and every reason to judge that we are responsible for them as far as personal responsibility goes in such a case.

But

III.

this narrative may teach us farther (and this is a brighter lesson) that in the darkest and most unpromising circumstances there is nearly always *some* way of relief and improvement. How seldom are things so in human life that literally nothing can be done! There is *something* unrepealable in all important human action. But there is also much that may be practically repealed. I think we may say that never, at any one time, in the history of a nation; never, in the life of an individual, are things so dark and bad that nothing can be done to amend and lighten them. On the contrary, this world, and the social and individual spheres of it, this whole mundane system, is constructed on the plan, so to say, of admitting, suggesting, prompting

to, and furnishing, the means of continual
recovery.

If this were not so, the world would soon
be full of the most pitiable spectacles that
could be conceived ; communities and individuals sitting hopelessly amid the gloom of
their own failures, amid the consequences of
their own mistakes, amid the deepening un-
happiness arising from the memory of their
own sins — the strokes of penalty heard
resounding on every side, the waters of
misery rising silently and coldly within, while
the long night of despair is deepening and
settling without.   Such pictures are not to
be seen.   There is indeed much suffering in
the world ; some of it penalty, and much of
it not.   And there are all kinds of calamities,
and mischances, and unexpected and unsuspected griefs, and things that ought never to
have happened, and things which fill you
with sympathy, and pain, and profound regret,
and perhaps indignation, as soon as you know
them.   And there are many mournful people
who make the worst of them ; or shall we say
the best of them, for they really seem to
find a kind of dismal enjoyment in seeing

how bad they are, and in anticipating that they are going to be still worse.

But who knows not, also, that calamities and misfortunes are retrieved, that injuries are redressed, that mistakes are rectified? Who knows not that oppressions come to an end, and bloody wars, and other evil works? Yes, and those things are accomplished sometimes just when everything appears almost hopeless, and by means which do not seem at all sufficient or equal to the end.

As Esther set her single will against the deadly edict, and drew from it, as far as her people were concerned, its deadliness, so a single will is often set against a whole system of evil, and by vigorous and persevering assaults it is brought to an end.

IV.

It is worth reflecting just for a few moments on the last clause of the last verse. "Many of the people of the land became Jews." It may indeed be questioned whether the adhesion of some of them was worth very much.

"The fear of the Jews fell on them." They were consulting for their own safety; they were not professing, from intelligence and conviction, a better religion. They saw the fate of Haman. They knew now that the queen was a Jewess, and the prime minister, and the king, of course, in these circumstances, in their favour. Why should they swim against wind and tide? Why should they not be safe? Why should they not make safety doubly sure by incorporating themselves with this strange, this indestructible, this irresistible, people? It may thus be that many of them, in becoming Jews, had no more in their minds than a prudent and politic regard for their own safety. Good Matthew Henry tries to abate the force of this view by connecting their decision with what goes before in the last verse, as well as with its final clause. "The Jews had joy and gladness, a feast and a good day, when the king's commandment and decree came. And because they showed themselves so happy in the ways of their God and under his protection, therefore the people of the land were drawn to them, and said, 'We will

go with you, for we have heard, and now we
see, that the Lord is with you.'" Then he
makes this general reflection, which no doubt
is true enough—"The holy cheerfulness of
those who profess religion is a great orna-
ment to their profession, and will invite and
encourage others to be religious." We shall
be safer to follow the narrative more closely,
and suppose that it was *the fear* of the Jews
much more than any admiration of them, or
any felt attraction by them, which made
these converts. But what then? Either
way it was a gain, although not so much in
one way as in the other.

V.

We hope it may not be considered an
anticlimax if we close this Lecture by asking
you to pay a tribute of thankfulness to the
four-footed creatures which were the really
effective executors of the king's decree of
salvation for the Jews. Without the aid of
these creatures it would have been impossible
to convey the tidings to some of the provinces
in time. Imperial man is, physically, and in

regard to locomotion, but a poor ineffective biped compared with the four-footed creatures here named—" the horse, the mule, the camel, the young dromedary." He can bridle and yoke the horse, and direct him whither he will ; but he could not himself run as swiftly or carry so much, or continue so long on the way. He can bestride the patient camel and tell the world that it is not so patient as it looks, that it has an evil temper. But no man could plod on for days across the desert of sand without water or food. He can shoot the eagle, but he could not fly across a narrow stream or chasm, if his life depended on it. So royal, so subject is man ! So strong, so weak. And therefore God has given him these helps of the other creatures exactly suited to his needs. Surely it does not require an argument to show that we ought to have very kindly feelings to these inferior, but most helpful creatures. *Very* helpful they were in this old Persian world. These "*posts*" mentioned in the chapter— these riders carrying letters on swift beasts, were historically very distinguished, as being probably the first fully-organised and equipped service of the kind in the world—the first, and one of the best that has ever been. Posts and couriers began in Persia,—so say the Greek writers—and reached great perfection there. Postal stations were on the ways to all the provinces. Solitary enough some of them would be in the sparsely peopled parts of the country. But horses and men were at each station. The posts travelled night and day, without intermission ; and the whole world stood astonished at the celerity with which edicts were carried to distant provinces ; and with which tidings from these provinces reached the capital again.

Certainly most helpful these creatures were on this occasion. " But surely we are not expected to throw gratitude back so far in history, and to creatures so long since perished and gone ? " Well, no, not in any lively form, certainly, but those creatures have left successors in the world ; and there cannot be many of us who are not served by them, more or less, almost every day. They carry our letters still, even in the city, and yet more, if we write to friends in out-of-the-

way places.   They carry our goods.   They
carry our persons.   While there are humbler
tribes and classes of the great animal creation,
that come about us on our invitation, simply
for our enjoyment.   They attend us for our
pleasure : we should see to it that it is not at
the sacrifice of their own.   " The merciful
man is merciful to his beast."   If, *i.e.*, he has
the really merciful disposition, the expressions
of it will not be confined to the members of
his own species.   It will go through *all* the
spheres of organised and sensitive existence.
In proportion as a nation grows, in thought-
fulness, in gentleness, in generosity, in justice,
the inferior creatures in that nation will feel
the benefit.   The feeling and habit we
commend is almost what we call the feeling
of humanity.   We quite acknowledge the
difference in the nature of the *objects* of our
compassion when we pity the oppressed, the
persecuted, the wounded in war, and when
we pity over-driven and half-famished horses,
some of them mercilessly abused by drivers,
or vivisected dogs.   But it is very difficult to
distinguish between the one feeling and the
other, at least at the point where they meet.

And there is no need to distinguish. We have this great fountain (great unless we make it small) of natural compassion in the breast—that we may pity all suffering—that we may be kind to all creatures.

Do we not know that this is a more *divine* feeling than many imagine, and lies closer along the line of our redemption? For what is our redemption, and how is it accomplished? Redemption is the mercifulness of God to man—pardoning, purifying, restoring him from sin and misery, and extending to him some small measure of his own divine felicity. Redemption is accomplished by the coming down of God among men. The acts of redemption are a series of condescensions— divine condescensions. God comes down into the world in the person of His Son. He comes down farther yet, into the individual heart, by the indwellings, and illuminations, and comfortings of the Spirit. He comes down into the lowliest ways of our life, by His providence, meeting us wherever we have need to be.

Nor is this all. He teaches the angels the same lesson. If they would help Him,

they can only do it in one way—they must
serve. " Are they not all ministering spirits?"
serving a race inferior to themselves.   Well,
we too, surely, must condescend and come
down—first to those of our fellow-creatures
of the human race who are beneath ourselves
in knowledge, in privilege, in virtue,—to the
" men of low estate," and then to the waiting,
serviceable, helpful creatures, treating them—
I shall not say mercifully only, but justly and
rightly.   We know nothing about the possible
immortality of any of the animal races or of
any individual specimens of the same.   See,
there is a shepherd who for years on those
hill-sides, grassy green in summer, snow-
white in winter, has had one faithful com-
panion in the keeping of the flock; and what
an attachment has sprung up between them,
and been growing silently through all those
years, it would surprise some people to know.
Well, the dog dies ; and the shepherd dies—
are we quite sure that they are never to meet
again ? and that there is not to be some
realisation, not of course in the rough form,
but in some refined form, of the Indian's
expectation—" that, when translated to that

equal sky, his faithful dog shall bear him company." But I say we know nothing of this—one way or other remember—and we found no obligation of man to the animal world on the basis of their possible immortality. No; their claim rests on what they are, on the nature they possess, on the sensibilities they evince, on the services they render, on the plans they respectively fill in this manifold, wonderful, interdependent, world and life. We cannot treat them cruelly or neglectfully, without violating what may be called "rights"—although the poor dumb creatures cannot plead them. In fact, in that way we show ourselves irreligious, unfaithful, unfilial; while by mercifulness and kindness we show ourselves the children of Him who, by the opening of His hand, satisfieth the desire of every living thing.

LECTURE XI.

CHAPTER IX. to the end of the book.

DEFENCE AND VICTORY OF THE JEWS.

THERE remains now not much to explain in this history; although *what* remains is eventful and tragical enough. The fated day came slowly on. "Light, and gladness, and joy, and honour," had come to the Jews, with the tidings of the decree passed in their favour giving them liberty of defence. But it is very likely that as the slow months rolled on, and the terrible 13th day of the month Adar drew near, they had their dark times of depression and apprehension. They could not be *quite* sure how the matter would turn out until the day had come and gone. The intervening months were spent, however, not in alarmed apprehension, but in wise and efficient preparation. None of the Jews seem to have fled out of the country. None were factious or timorous. They drew together in the respective cities and districts, put themselves under strict discipline, and prepared themselves for the sternest resistance if it should be necessary.

And it *was* necessary. For, strange to say, although the tide has now so completely turned in favour of the Jews, there seems no abatement at all corresponding, or such as might be expected, in the hostility and hatred of a considerable part of the population of the Persian Empire. Haman, the author of the edict of blood, gone! the queen a Jewess! the prime minister a Jew! the king adopting their policy,—these are very strong circumstances,—which no doubt produced due effect on the official classes everywhere. They would all but certainly go with the policy of the second edict. They would naturally and excusably be on the side of the prevailing influence. Yet, notwithstanding all this, there seems left quite a large body of the Persians filled with unquench-

able hatred of this strange people called
Jews ; and who are preparing to carry out
the *first* edict to its bloodiest issues as far as
their power may go. We have not any
specific declarations to this effect. But the
facts show this beyond all question. For we
must remember that the Jews were not
allowed to assail their enemies unprovoked,
but only to defend themselves by resisting
and even attacking those who are preparing
to assail and destroy them. In these circumstances, that so many should have been slain
by the Jews, shows that their assailants
must have been numerous, and that their
antipathies must have been indeed strong.
No doubt, as the history tells us, "the
enemies of the Jews hoped to have power
over them." "But it was turned to the contrary "—as mischievous and cruel plans so
often are. The Jews "gathered themselves
together :" stood for their life : laid hands
on those who would have assaulted them ;
were helped by rulers, lieutenants, deputies,
officers—by the whole civil service of the
country, while the name of the great minister
Mordecai stood like a tower of strength to

them. And the result was that 500 men were slain in the capital, in Shushan the palace, and throughout the whole empire 75,000 men! This is the military result of the conflict, and a very dreadful result it is to come from one man's malignity and pride. Some rationalistic writers have called in question the truth of this narrative, founding their objection to it chiefly on the somewhat astounding character of these figures, 75,000 all slain by a handful of people; and not one Jew slain! Nay, the narrative does not say that no Jews fell. It passes the matter by in silence. But the certainty, we should say, is that *some* of the Jews fell. The probability is that a moderate number of the Jewish combatants died in the ignoble strife, —for it was street-fighting—barricade-work, or something analogous, such as excitable people betake themselves to in times of revolution.

Then as to the numbers slain by the Jews, let us see if there be anything incredible in the statement. Consider the size of the great Persian kingdom; and that it must have contained at this time at least a hundred millions of people. The number of Jews, it is thought, could not have been much less than three millions. Three million people could send out 500,000 men easily, capable of bearing arms. And it is not at all incredible, that in the kind of fighting we have referred to, where their enemies being the assailants, would be exposed and at a disadvantage, 75,000 should fall. Shushan the capital was about the size of a very famous city of our own day—Stamboul or Constantinople—it held half a million of people. Would there be anything incredible in hearing that 500 men had fallen in street-fighting, if such a thing should break out? Surely not. But sceptical critics always treat the Bible more hardly in the matter of evidence than other books, and unless the proof be overwhelming, which it generally is however, they quietly assume that, in some way, a great mistake has occurred.

75,000! A terrible death-list—containing who knows how many affecting instances of bereavement, and sorrow, and distress.

Among the rest fell the ten sons of Haman, which is affecting enough in some aspects.

True they seem to have courted, and *merited* therefore, the fate which thus overtakes them. If they had not been fighting of their own will and choice, they would not have been slain. They were probably chiefs and ring-leaders of the Hamanist or anti-Jewish faction, and as they voluntarily rush forward into the dangers of the strife, they must take the chances of the war, and meet their fate, as I daresay they did, bravely and without complaining. Yet, surely, that fate is a pitiful one ! Ten of them !—and all in strong bright youth and manhood ! And possessors of such names —speaking as those names do of the father's and mother's pride in them ! and love for them ! and hope concerning them ! They are all slain—and then not buried even with the soldier's hasty burial—but to fix on them the deepest stigma and disgrace—they are hung ! Probably this was done, as some of the commentators suggest, partly as a warning to the enemies of the Jews, and might thus operate to the saving of human life. But there can be no doubt that it was also done passionately and spitefully. It does not do —I mean it is not quite safe for ourselves to be too ingenious in finding the most favourable explanations of doubtful things, because they are done by the people of God. For our own souls' health and magnanimity it is necessary to say that—while we do not judge of circumstances unknown to us, and of the worth of reasons which are not written down —we do see and think that hanging up ten young men in this way after they were dead —it is said one above another—is in itself a small, mean, malignant thing—in its nature too much like the spirit of that very Haman whose name they wished to blot out from the earth.

On the other side of the account this— that with emphasis it is stated that in Shushan the palace, in a great city, they slew 500 *men.* Twice it is said they slew *only men.* They were allowed to slay women and children. But as this was not necessary to their own preservation, they took the course dictated by humanity and mercy. And this stands well to their credit.

It might seem perhaps to some that Esther herself was lacking in this humanity, when, using her great influence over her uxorious husband, and in reply to his desire to know what *now* she wished further done, assuring her that her wish should immediately be royal command — she asked not only that Haman's sons should be hanged — but that there might be *another* day of slaughter added to the first. One very vigorous objector speaks of it as "another day of butchery in the palace." But that is mere excess and exaggeration. The whole meaning of Esther's prayer is that the Jews might be allowed to continue the defence for another day, since the assault had not yet ceased.

The request was wholly reasonable, and it was at once granted. It was only in the palace, *i.e.* in the capital city, that this was necessary; throughout the provinces of the empire the fighting began and ended on the same day.

Then came the institution of the feast of Purim, intended to be, as it has been, commemorative of the great and terrible danger through which this whole nation passed, and of the signal and happy deliverance wrought for them in the good providence of God. "The feast of Purim"—*i.e.* the feast of lots;

for the Persic word " pur" signifies " the lot." The lot was cast "into the lap" of time, for their destruction, but the whole disposing thereof was of the Lord for their preservation and deliverance ; and now they decree to keep a yearly feast in memory of these things, and that it shall be a perpetual feast through all their generations. It *has* been so kept ; it is so kept at this day. The separate existence of the Jews at this day is some proof of the truth of the Scripture history concerning them. The existence and observance of this feast among them still is a proof of the truth of that particular part of their history which is written in this book.

We are now at the end of our exposition of the book. A word or two may be said of the persons described in the book who are still living at the end of the history.

AHASUERUS.

The King Ahasuerus is (as you will re-member we concluded) none other than the great Persian monarch Xerxes, who invaded Greece, and met with signal defeat and humiliation there. The whole character of *that* monarch agrees well with what we read of Ahasuerus in this book of Esther. He built a bridge over the Hellespont—that famous Hellespont where mighty nations are meeting, and watching, and striving still. The elements destroyed it, and he caused the engineers who constructed it to be beheaded. The sea misbehaved on a stormy day, and he had it scourged and fettered by sinking chains in it! He dishonoured the remains of the valiant Leonidas. He offered a reward to the inventor of a new pleasure. It is the very man who deposes Vashti for resisting his drunken freak of vanity ; who yields to Esther because she is beautiful ; who sits down to drink with Haman after signing the death-warrant of three millions of his own subjects ; who says to Mordecai, "As it liketh you"—"get out of the difficulty as best you can."

He came to an end which suits but too darkly well with his character and life : he was murdered in the year B.C. 465, by one who aspired to the throne and did not reach it, for he was succeeded by his son Artaxerxes. Pass away from our view, thou arch pretender to greatness ; thou kingly shadow without kingly substance ; thou abject slave wearing a monarch's dress ! Go to the grave that will never be softened with the tears or touched with the feet of mourners ; while we wonder how one so vain and empty and bad as thou could ever, even *outwardly*, play so large a part in the history of the world !

HAMAN'S WIFE.

Haman is gone, and his ten sons, and we need say no more of them ; but Haman's wife, it is said, survived—survived to think sadly of her once famous husband, of her stalwart sons, all swept away from her in a storm of ruin and disgrace !—survived to be forgotten or neglected by the fair-weather friends who once had esteemed it their pride to be among her guests !—survived to be poor, and hungry, and in utter want. 'Tis said she was found one day begging her bread. Let us hope that, in the bitter school of adversity and calamity like hers, she at length learned to be merciful, to be womanly, and to look on to a world in which, if we rightly

R

enter it, all sorrow may have compensation
and all misfortune be retrieved.

MORDECAI.

There is a Mordecai mentioned as having
returned to Jerusalem under Zerubbabel, but
it is agreed that it could not be the Mordecai
of this book.   It is far more likely that he
stayed where he was.   A man of transcendent
political ability, he might judge himself more
in his place where he was ; better situated for
doing good to his people and the great cause
of God in the world than if he had returned
to Jerusalem.   The book of Esther closes
with a high testimony in his favour. A clearer
and finer testimony hardly could be given,
as far as it goes.   "He was great."   Ah !
how that word "greatness" is often misused
and debased !   A man bears a certain name,
and therefore he is great ; or he wears a certain robe, and therefore he is great ; or he
succeeds in slaughtering an immense number
of his fellow-creatures, and therefore he is
great ; or by much cunning, and audacity, and
cleverness withal, he keeps himself in con-

spicuous place and before the eyes of his fellow-countrymen, and therefore he is great!

Not such a greatness as any of these was that of Mordecai. It was a greatness won, no doubt, by his splendid faculty of management, by his statesmanship, but, with real substance in it of truth and goodness. He was great, not only as at the practical head of the government of this great empire of Persia, but he was so esteemed among "his own people," who were despised and persecuted as they so often have been, and who numbered not more than one in thirty of the population. He "*sought the wealth of his people.*" Jewish-like, no doubt, is this; but observe, it was *his people's* wealth, not *his own*, he sought. And the last word concerning him on record is this, that "he spake peace to all his seed." He was accessible, he was gentle, he was generous and patriotic, promoting the well-being of his seed, but not at the expense of the country in which he was born. Would that all who are in great place in our own country, and in this our own day, would follow very literally Mordecai's example and speak "peace."

ESTHER.

We part from her also on like terms of thankfulness and admiration. There are things, of course, about the court life and the social life of that time which we abhor, and in which Esther is mixed up. But in character and action she herself, as far as we can see, is pure, and brave, and noble ; and she continues so to the end. The last of her public acts *recorded* is the confirmation of the decree called by her own name, by which this famous feast of Purim would be kept in the families and along the generations of the Jews, as it is this day. An affecting memorial of the wonderful goodness of divine providence to them, a yearly stimulus to gratitude, a yearly help to prayerfulness and trust. Pass *thou* away from our sight, O queen, in unsullied beauty of true queenliness, in purity, in honour, in unselfishness. " Many daughters have done virtuously," and if we cannot say that " thou excellest them all," we can say that thou standest well forward among the best. We know not what, farther, in this earthly life shall happen to thee, or where thy lot will be cast. But we feel sure that the wonderful and kindly providence that watched over thine orphanage, and made thee a queen, the greatest queen in the world, and this for the attainment of some of the greatest ends, will not forsake thee now, but will in some way make thee a blessing to thy people to the end.

Now there are many general lessons and inferences, taken from the book in its wholeness, on which we might easily enlarge. We can select only a few of these, and give them but a brief illustration :—

I.

A book like this of Esther, bringing before us, as it does, in very vivid portraiture, the state of the things in the foremost kingdom of the world in that long ago time, enables us to see, at least in some respects, *what progress the world has made since then.* We mean especially in the highest and best things. This world's progress is a manifold thing, composed of a great variety of elements ; and it has not gone on by graduated steps, and as through an evolutionary devel-

opment, without failure, recession, or reverse.
On the contrary, there have been many
alternations ; there has been much loss. There
are lost arts, and refinements and conveniences
of life have been lost, and books and MSS.
of great worth. There has not been always
gain ; and the gain has not been unmixed.
But there has been gain on the whole, and,
as we have said, especially in the highest
things. In regard to all that is comprised
under the great phrase, "*civil and religious
liberty*," the world, on the whole, is now farther forward than it has ever been before.
All the splendours of the Persian court, and
all the pomps and pleasures of that ancient
Eastern life, will not bear comparison with
the great things of Christendom and of our
Christian life—honour, virtue, truth, religion
in its twofold form of the love of God and
the love of man—these, and such like things,
are the fruits and proofs of this world's progress in the higher sense. And although they
are much mixed and darkly shaded and
environed at present by their opposites—
meanness, falsehood, cruelty, tyranny, licen-
tiousness, hatreds, envyings, strifes, in social,

national, and international life—yet are they things which cannot die, because they have come directly from God through Jesus Christ, who therefore will keep such things living, growing, multiplying, according to His promise, until they leaven the whole human race and regenerate the whole world.

We know it might be objected to this view of things that the moral providence of God described in this book of Esther, as it affects all the chief characters, seems to be really a more perfect instrument than the providence of this day. And one can imagine a man, sadly, after looking at some of the darker parts of life among ourselves, in social, commercial, political, international things, saying, " Ah, would that we had such a providence among men and nations now— especially among ourselves to-day. The very providence that overthrew Haman, and lifted Mordecai and Esther, and saved an innocent people—a providence, sharp-eyed, swift-footed, heavy-handed—to strike down, to lift up ; to kill, to make alive ! " One might answer—" We *sometimes* have still in this tumultuous, tempestuous, ever-changing

life, things not so unlike the book of Esther
in celerity, unexpectedness, tragic pathos, and
grandeur." No one has the right to suppose
that God is managing the progress of this
world so that He may increasingly retire from
it. That were a wretched boon to the world.
Now and again, " by terrible things in righteousness," and, by beautiful and joyful things
in mercy, He makes His very *presence* known
among men. But the true answer to such
a reflection as that we have referred to
is this, that the moral providence of God
over nations and individuals now is a far
finer and more perfect instrument, so to say,
than that which we see working in the life of
Esther, or Ruth, or David, or Daniel. It is
a providence of principles calmly working
towards certain issues : a providence that
flows on more evenly now, fed from its fountains of fulness and perfection in God : a
providence of divine power and grace, which
will secure at length the highest possible progress and perfection of the world and man.

And finally, we shall miss what is perhaps
the most precious teaching of this book if,

observing and thankful for such general progress in civil and religious things, we make this
in any way a substitute for the full sense we
ought always to have, of *the presence and
action of a personal God.* There is no need
to say, for every thoughtful well-read person
knows it, that the tendency, in our time, is
very strong to resolve the living God into
—progressive providence, into general laws,
into moral government. Not so much the
spirit of ungodliness is leading men to this,
as the spirit of philosophy and the findings
of science—or, to put it perhaps more cor-
rectly, the spirit of the new philosophies inter-
preting the findings of science. " It is not a
vital matter," they say, how the great realities
are put : it is very much a matter of human
conception and individual taste : *conduct* may
be equally good either way—whether we say
" a great infinite power in the universe which
makes for righteousness," or—" the living and
true God "—whether we say " Force, material
and moral force, is king ;" or " Jehovah is
king." This is a phase of human thought
which can only be met by strong argument, fair statements, and patient waiting ;

never by strong language simply. We must not say to the philosophers any more than to one another, " The adversary and enemy is this wicked Haman." Those whose opinions we controvert, and whose influence in one particular line we would lessen, are not wicked, are in fact in some respects very honest and true, slightly irreverent perhaps, not strong in the religious faculty, given to pry into physical mysteries, and to assume that there are no mysteries or realities beyond, and to assume also that some new definitions will explain them—but not wicked, and therefore never to be made the subjects of " railing " or even gentle " accusation."

But because there are scientists, and physical truth-seekers in the world now, who have gone farther into the darkness of nature than men ever went before, saying by their very discoveries in some inferior sense—" Let there be light "—are we no longer to believe in the God of our fathers? In " the God and Father of our Lord Jesus Christ "? This book of Esther teaches this above all things, that God is near to all that call upon Him, to all who call upon Him in truth, and that

He is always working for the protection of
those who really trust in Him, and for the
advancement of every right cause, and for
the punishment of evil-doers, and for the
confusion of every evil work. He took the
little orphan-girl by the hand, and at last
made her a queen! He lifted the keeper of
the king's gate, and set him over all the provinces of the empire! He hurled the proud
and revengeful Amalekite from the heights
of power to the depths of shame! By a
sleepless night, and recollections of a deliverance produced accidentally in the king's
mind, He wrought out His own will in firm
texture. And "this God is our God for ever
and ever." He has not left the world since
then, is not any farther away from it, has
surely drawn it a little nearer to Himself.
The daylight is more and not less His smile.
The darkness is *more* the shadow of His
wings. There are even select ones who so
share His own thought and love and life
that they have their human part of His high
experience in finding " the darkness and the
light both alike alway." And the summer
is His beauty. And the autumn is His

generosity. And human kindness springs up under the very breath of His nearness; while all His deeper thoughts are told out to us in the gift of His dear Son. Still He is the strength of the worker; and the rest of the weary. Still doth His hand wipe away the mourner's tears. Still, and for ever, in His tireless love He is about the ways of all who do not by black unbelief shut Him out of their life. It concerns us, infinitely far beyond all mortal concernments, that we shut Him not out of ours.

THE END.

Printed by R. & R. CLARK, *Edinburgh.*

By the Same.

NINTH EDITION.

In One Volume, Crown 8vo, Price 7s. 6d.

Quiet Resting Places

AND OTHER SERMONS.

Contemporary Review.

Full of exquisite beauty of thought and language ; sometimes bordering on the fanciful in their application of texts, but even then never going beyond the limits of good taste and simple pathos. The title of the Volume is taken from the text of the first sermon, and it well describes the character of the book. Dr. Raleigh specially seeks out the indications given in the divine promises of rest and refreshment, and pursues them into their fulfilments in the ordinary life of the Christian.

British Quarterly Review.

Sermons of great beauty and power, such as rarely issue from the press. We can only wish them the widest possible circulation.

Eclectic Review.

We must lay down this volume ; it cannot be less delightful than useful. We have quoted sufficiently to show that the reader will find, in almost any page, a quiet resting-place in its short graphic pictures, and revealings of homes and hearts, in its pensive but never merely sentimental stillness, in its, we had almost said, robust language, and its healthful views of life and religion.

Record.

The word "sermons" prefixed to a book serves more as a warning than an attraction to the majority of readers. We must plead guilty to sharing in this feeling, and are therefore the more bound to acknowledge the gratification we have had, the profit and pleasure we should rather say, in reading this volume. Thoroughly evangelical truth is taught with the freshness of thought and expression of one who has himself drawn the living water from the fountain-head. It is just the book to place in the hands of young people, of whom there are too many in the present day who have taken up the foolish prejudice that beauty of style and nobleness of thought are only to be found in conjunction with errors. As a matter of literary taste, we greatly admire Mr. Raleigh's style. It is not a string of illustrations, and yet it is rich. It is perfectly intelligible, without any affectation of simplicity. And as you read the book, you cannot help thinking more of the substance than the manner, with the consciousness, all the while, that you are carried along on a stream of pleasant words. It is of no use to make extracts, but we strongly advise our readers to buy "Quiet Resting Places" for themselves.

Sheffield Independent.

Those of our readers who have heard the Author need not be told they are admirable specimens of thoroughly-reasoned discourses, opening up the Scriptures on which they are founded with marvellous skill, clearness, and fulness. There is nothing commonplace in them, but every one is replete with fresh and earnest thought—thought so thrilling and vitalising, that their effect is anything but quiet-giving. They evoke thought and emotion, and cannot be read without drawing out the reader to immediate and determined action.

Western Daily Press.

We have not, indeed, met with sermons to be compared with Mr. Raleigh's for exquisite and delicate forms of thought and imagination. Rigid criticism may be applied to them without any other result than unqualified admiration. As mere compositions, they excite surprise by the minute and patient finish, by the polished thought, as well as by the apt and striking words employed. Their higher qualities we leave the reader to judge of by the extracts which we add.

Christian Times.

We have read these sermons, and, rising from their perusal, our first impulse is to thank God that they have been preached and printed.

Patriot.

Great and almost perfect as is their literary beauty, this is not their chief characteristic ; they are full of spiritual sensibility and purpose ; they aim supremely, and in every paragraph, at what should be the end of all preaching, the spiritual edification of the hearers. But the literary finish and beauty of the sermons are so remarkable that none can fail to be arrested by them. Every sentence is poetically conceived and artistically chiselled. He has bestowed infinite pains to make things simple. He is a consummate artist in words. How beautiful the form is into which his thoughts are put will be seen in the extracts that we subjoin.

Our Own Fireside.

The third edition of this volume indicates that a portion of the public, at least, have rightly estimated its value ; but we confess a " third " edition is far from satisfactory.   Religious books, weak and vapid in character, are too often widely circulated, while such works as this, for example, only reach the thoughtful few.   It will not be our fault if our readers do not enrich their libraries, if they have not already done so, with " Quiet Resting Places. " We have inserted one of the chapters in our present part—" The House of Obed-edom "—as a specimen of twenty other chapters or sermons treating of topics of absorbing interest.   Every page of this volume bears the impress of a sound mind, judicious amidst its originality, and truly reverential, notwithstanding its independence ; and we should regard it as a token for good if the " third " edition speedily became the " thirtieth. "

EDINBURGH : ADAM AND CHARLES BLACK.

By the Same.
In One Volume, Illustrated, Price 3s. 6d.

THE

Story of Jonah the Prophet.

British Quarterly Review.

It is hardly possible to speak too highly of the dramatic force, the historic imagination, the brilliancy and piquancy with which our author has made this old-world story live again. He has produced a photograph of the prophet, and has analysed his character and mental development with an insight and sympathy approaching to genius ; and difficult as the task has been, he has, we think, with few exceptions, brought us in his treatment of the narrative face to face with God. The three chapters entitled "The Flight," "Sailed," "The Storm," convey to us the impression of great power, and we reckon them among the most impressive sermons that we have ever read. The felicitous diction, the masterly exegesis, the dexterous application of the principles that are evolved to modern life, and dangers, and controversy, and the moral power of the closing appeals to the conscience, give these discourses superlative merit. The closing discourse, entitled "Selah," contains passages of great beauty and suggestiveness ; and the volume as a whole is one of the most practical and morally earnest that we have ever read.

Record.

We have already had occasion to speak in high terms of the published sermons of Dr. Raleigh, and the present volume fully bears out our favourable opinion, both as to its style and matter.

THE STORY OF JONAH—*Continued.*

Eclectic Review.

This new volume from the pen of Dr. Raleigh will more than sustain the reputation of the author of " Quiet Resting Places ; " its appearance is about the most remarkable we ever remember to have found associated with a volume of sermons, and appeals quite as much to the *recherché* tastes of the drawing-room table as its matter conducts to the oratory or the study ; the illuminations at the opening of each discourse ; the map upon the title-page ; the sketches from the antique ; the tinted frontispiece illustrating Jonah's traditional tomb—all give to the volume an appearance of artistic elegance which certainly should not be unnoticed in the introduction of the volume to our readers. . . . . . Here, then, we do not so much bid farewell to Dr. Raleigh as introduce his volume to our readers, assuring them that throughout its pages it shines with the same subdued splendour of speech, and melts with the same pathos of feeling, as in those passages we have quoted.

Freeman.

The qualities of the book, that strike even a cursory observer, are the beauty of the thought, the clearness and directness of the style, the manly strong sense displayed in the views given of mysterious truth, and the reverent, earnest spirit that pervades the whole. We might quote from each of the fourteen chapters of the volume—every passage affording instruction and exciting delight.

Patriot.

The present volume is sure to enhance his high reputation. It has all the richness of thought, the felicity of illustration, the wonderful charm of style, and the warm glow of devout and holy feelings by which its predecessor was distinguished ; and, combined with these, a large infusion of elements in which it was somewhat deficient. Dr. Raleigh is a master of word-painting. In many points he reminds us of Dr. Guthrie, with whom he has not unfrequently been compared. He has, however, a more thorough control of his own powers than the great Free Church divine. There is less gorgeousness, but there is more simplicity, naturalness, quiet and chastened beauty. His book is sure to be popular.

Christian Witness.

We are carried forward from page to page, from chapter to chapter, of the "Story of Jonah" with scarcely a consciousness of time or of labour. Everything is so simple, so clear, so natural, and therefore so beautiful, that we forget both the writer and his style, and become absorbed in the facts and the thoughts themselves.

Nonconformist.

In every page do the preacher's well-known devoutness, taste, and skill appear. His pictorial power and his fine sympathy, which intuitively appreciates the subtler as well as the more obvious suggestions of each moral scene, find ample occasion and scope in the strange history of Jonah. We are very sure the book will be widely read, and we are glad that Dr. Raleigh speaks through so instructive and impressive a volume to the churches of our land.

EDINBURGH : ADAM AND CHARLES BLACK.

www.ingramcontent.com/pod-product-compliance
Lightning Source LLC
Chambersburg PA
CBHW020352030726
47496CB00007B/2112